PRAISE FOR
ZARA HOSSAIN IS HERE

★ "[*Zara Hossain Is Here*] establishes Khan as **a powerful rising voice in YA**." —*Booklist*, starred review

"Fans of Samira Ahmed, Tahereh Mafi, and Randa Abdel-Fattah will find Khan's powerful work **timely and affecting**."
—*School Library Journal*

★ "Khan **unapologetically tackles prejudice** in its various manifestations, challenging readers to ask what it means for some to feel at home in a country whose systems feel built to exclude them." —*Kirkus Reviews*, starred review

"Khan creates a **gripping** story line centering the conflict between prejudice and tolerance." —*Publishers Weekly*

PRAISE FOR
THE LOVE & LIES OF RUKHSANA ALI

A Junior Library Guild Selection
An ALA-YALSA Quick Picks for Young Adult Readers Book
A Rainbow Book List Top Ten Book of the Year

"Rukhsana's character courageously captures what today's queer teen Muslim experience can look like." —*Teen Vogue*

"Equal parts **heart-wrenching, impactful, and hopeful**."
—BuzzFeed

"An **intersectional, diverse coming of age story** that will break your heart in the best way." —Bustle

★ "With an up-close depiction of the intersection of the LGBTQIA+ community with Bengali culture, this **hard-hitting and hopeful** story is a must-purchase for any YA collection."
—*School Library Journal*, starred review

"[*The Love and Lies of Rukhsana Ali*] **takes LGBTQ fiction to another level** and will help open readers' eyes to the realities that many face in these changing times." —Shelf Awareness

"This **moving** novel offers readers a deep look into Bengali traditions and dreams for a more inclusive future, with a resilient girl at the heart of it." —*Booklist*

"Told tenderly and unflinchingly, balancing the horrors of homophobia against the South Asian men and women who risk their lives to fight it each and every day." —*Kirkus Reviews*

"Sabina Khan crafts a **powerful, poignant story** about finding yourself, about speaking your truth, and about stepping out of the shadows and into the light." —Samira Ahmed, *New York Times* bestselling author of *Love, Hate and Other Filters* and *Internment*

"This book will break your heart and then, chapter by chapter, piece it back together again. **A much-needed addition to any YA shelf.**" —Sandhya Menon, *New York Times* bestselling author of *When Dimple Met Rishi* and *From Twinkle, with Love*

"**Bold, heartbreaking, yet hopeful.** A story that will stay with you for years to come." —Sara Farizan, author of the Lambda Award–winning novel *If You Could Be Mine* and *Here to Stay*

"Political, personal, page turning. **Sabina Khan is one to watch.**" —Tanuja Desai Hidier, author of *Born Confused* and *Bombay Blues*

"Khan brings talent and voice in this **brilliant** novel that will keep you reading until the very last page." —Nisha Sharma, author of *My So-Called Bollywood Life*

Sabina Khan

Scholastic Inc.

Copyright © 2021 by Sabina Khan

This book was originally published in hardcover by Scholastic Press in 2021.

ISBN 978-1-338-81962-5

1 2021

Printed in the U.S.A.   23
This edition first printing 2022
Book design by Maeve Norton

CX 11 02 2021 0307

To all those who leave home for
a better world.
To Jaanu, forever my home.
To my greatest pride and joy,
Sonya and Sanaa.
And to my beloved Nikki, who fills
my world with light.

CHAPTER ONE

Inhale. Exhale. Repeat.

I focus on each breath, pushing the anger to the back of my mind. It's nothing new, this need to punch something, to rage at the world. This is my reality and I'm used to it. That almost angers me more than the actual microaggressions I deal with daily. I concentrate on each pattern as I step, kick, and punch, chasing that elusive feeling of peace. Finally, it's there, the calm after the storm, and I stop to catch my breath.

Mr. Clair's last class of the day is just finishing up, so the students are filing out of the rec center.

"Hey, Zara, I haven't seen you here for a while," he says, stacking the last of the boards and placing them inside the cabinet. He was my tae kwon do instructor for years, ever since I was six and just starting out.

I'm glad Abbu didn't let me quit after I got my green belt. I remember being so frustrated when I didn't pass the exam the first time that I just wanted to stop. But Abbu would help me with my patterns and Ammi would quiz me on the tenets: courtesy, integrity, perseverance, self-control, and indomitable spirit.

It didn't help that I used to be terrified of Mr. Clair and that every time he looked at me I turned into a noodle. These days we can both laugh about it. I still go there sometimes to help him out with the white belts. But on days like today, when I feel like I might lose control, it's a sanctuary.

"I've just been super busy with school," I reply. I want this space to be free of all the other stuff in my life right now. Mr. Clair knows my family well, given that all three of us spent a great deal of time here up until I was fifteen. That's when I finally got my black belt.

I give him a hand with the sliding room divider, and then we start. He goes easy on me at first, just a few basic jump kicks, axe kicks, and hook kicks. Then he steps it up, and I have to watch out. I use a roundhouse kick as bait. I step into the maneuver, anticipating his counter. But I continue to spin, executing a perfect hook kick. Just like he taught me.

He throws me a smile. "I see you haven't forgotten. Good."

I smile back. "Thanks for letting me hang out."

He waves his hand dismissively. "You know you're welcome anytime."

I step out into the night and wait for Abbu to pick me up. My blouse sticks to my skin, and my hair has morphed into a giant ball of frizz in the eighty-degree heat of this humid evening. Just because I'm used to living in a perpetual sauna doesn't mean I like it. At all. Abbu's BMW rolls up, and I slide in gratefully to let the coolness from the air-conditioning vent blast in my face.

"Thanks for picking me up," I say, leaning over to give him a quick peck on the cheek.

"I was just on my way home, so it worked out perfectly," he says. "Did Ammi need the car today?"

I nod silently, looking out the window. It's almost nine o'clock, but it's still a little light out. Wherever I end up moving for college next year, I want to go someplace with *actual* seasons.

"What's the matter, beta?" Abbu looks at me before checking his backup camera as he pulls out of the parking lot. "You look tense. Everything okay at school?"

It's not, but I don't want to worry him. On the other hand, he'll worry more if I don't tell him.

"Things have been weird lately," I begin, still hesitant to confide in him.

"Weird how, beta?" Abbu turns on South Staples, passing a row of apartment buildings and a Circle K.

"Just some kids at school. They've been saying stuff lately. Stupid things about Muslims."

The light turns yellow, then red, and Abbu brings the car to a stop. He turns to me, concern deepening the lines on his forehead.

"Zara, you have to tell us these things," he says.

"I don't want you to be scared every time I go to school. You know how Ammi gets."

"Yes, beta, I know," Abbu says. The light turns green, and we're moving again. "But we need to know what's happening. You know how quickly things can get out of hand."

"I know, Abbu. And I promise I'll tell you."

"But let's just keep it between us," he says. "No need to worry your mother."

The peace I felt is gone now.

The truth?

I worry enough for all of us.

CHAPTER TWO

"Zara. Zaaarrraaa. Come down and eat breakfast."

Ammi's shrill voice carries up from the kitchen, into my bedroom and beyond. I won't be at all surprised if our neighbors are lined up by our front door expecting breakfast.

"Coming, Ammi," I call before she starts shouting again. I put on the finishing touches of eyeliner, dragging out the ends into wings. A dab of pink lip gloss, then I select a pair of large silver hoops from the crystal bowl on my dresser, grab my bag, and go downstairs.

My bichon puppy, Zorro, follows me, forever my shadow. Ammi is at the kitchen island preparing lunches for Abbu and me while simultaneously keeping an eye on the stove. I walk up to her and kiss her on the cheek.

"Good morning, Ammi." I hug her, tucking back a few errant strands of hair behind her ear before settling on a stool at the breakfast counter. She smiles and places a plate of steaming paranthay and scrambled eggs on the embroidered place mat in front of me.

"Good morning, meri chanda." She hands me a steaming

mug of coffee. I take it from her and breathe in the deep hazelnut aroma before taking a sip.

"Is your abbu coming down or what?" Ammi asks, sliding another parantha onto the platter. "His breakfast is getting cold."

She pours herself a cup of coffee and sits down on the stool next to me, the flowing sleeves of her silk kaftan brushing softly against my bare arms.

"Iqbaaaal!" she screams without warning, and the sound sends shock waves through my entire body. It's hard to believe that such a tiny person possesses a vocal power of nuclear proportions.

"So, anything exciting planned for today, Ammi?" I tear off a piece of parantha, use it to scoop up some scrambled eggs, and pop it in my mouth. Mmm. Heaven.

"Yes, Zara, I have a very exciting day planned for myself. Dishes, groceries, all so thrilling."

"Okay, Ammi, I get it." I grin at her as I finish up my eggs quickly before sliding off the stool. "I'll do the dishes right now." I begin to clear the kitchen island.

"Thank you, Zara. Actually, I was hoping to organize the study a little today."

I look up from loading the dirty plates into the dishwasher. "It's Tuesday. Don't you have book club today?"

"Yes, that's tonight. I hope that Shireen has actually read the book this time. Sometimes I think she only comes for my carrot halwa."

A couple of years ago, Ammi started a book club with a few of her friends. There's really not much else to do in Corpus Christi for a Muslim immigrant from Pakistan with a love for reading. Her social group includes the only two other Muslim women she knows in Corpus and Meredith, a colleague from the local library where Ammi works part-time. They pick books mostly by South Asian authors and discuss them over chai and delectable Pakistani snacks. I love Tuesdays mainly because I can stuff my face with chaat, samosas, and halwas. And, of course, the aunties. They're my trusty source for anything Bollywood.

Abbu finally walks into the kitchen and grabs a few bites of parantha and egg, while Ammi fusses over his tie.

"Iqbal, when will you listen to me and slow down? Your patients will still be there, even if you take ten minutes to eat a proper breakfast." My mom pours coffee into his travel mug before handing it to him, then disappears into the pantry. We can hear her grumbling to herself inside.

"I don't know why I bother to make a nice hot breakfast for you if you're just going to gobble it down," she complains to the neatly stacked containers of rice, lentils, and canned soups on the shelves. She emerges with a couple of Ziploc bags of trail mix. Abbu obediently takes one, as do I. It's easier than arguing with her.

"Nilufer, don't forget, I'll be late coming home today," Abbu reminds her, grabbing his stethoscope off the coffee table and stuffing it into his briefcase. "I have that dinner with the new partner, remember?" He kisses Ammi on the forehead before he heads out the door.

"Zara, beta, what's happening at school?" Ammi says, finally sitting down to finish her coffee. "Your father told me you seemed really upset last night."

I will never understand why either of my parents pretend they can actually keep secrets. They have to tell each other absolutely everything. It's kind of sweet except that now I know Ammi will worry.

"It's nothing, Ammi," I say dismissively. "Just some ignorant jerks. Nothing I can't handle."

She looks at me, her dark eyes full of concern. "Beta, I'm always scared these days. With everything on the news lately . . . things are changing and you have to be careful."

I hate that she feels like this. We have lived in Corpus Christi for fourteen years now, eight of them waiting to get our green cards. My parents brought me here with them from Pakistan when I was three so Abbu could start his pediatric residency. Eventually the hospital where he's worked for years agreed to sponsor his green card application, but we knew it could take years. We're almost at the end of the arduous process now, and the lawyer said we should expect to have our permanent resident status in just a few more months. It can't come soon enough since I graduate at the end of this school year and don't want to have to apply to college as an international student. We're a little afraid to be too optimistic, but I can't help feeling hopeful. It's what keeps me sane while I deal with idiots at school like Tyler Benson, aka jock, racist, moron.

I'd be lying if I said I don't worry sometimes when I'm at school. Tyler and his buddies certainly don't make any effort to hide how they really feel. As the only Muslim at school, I'm well aware that their comments are aimed at me. I just choose to ignore them, because the majority of the students are pretty great despite their homogeneity.

Most of the students at Our Lady of Perpetual Succour High School are Catholic. Then there's a handful of us heathens, I mean non-Catholics, at the school. There's Priya, whose family is from Kerala. Her father is an anesthesiologist and works with Abbu. Then there's Divya from Mumbai, whose mom is an engineer, and Andy from Taiwan, whose dad works in IT. Finally there's me, a Muslim girl from Pakistan.

Of course, there's also my best friend, Nick Garcia, who is

third-generation Mexican American and a star on our school's football team. I see him standing by the lockers waiting for me as he does every morning. He gets here early for football practice most days. Other days, Abbu gives us both a ride since we live only two houses down from each other. He's like the brother I never knew I wanted. We've been best friends ever since I crashed my bike in front of his house when I was five.

"Hey, there you are," he says after I drop my bag on the floor with a loud thump.

"Did you finish the chem assignment after I left yesterday?" I ask, pulling out my textbook for first period.

"I tried, but I got, you know, distracted," he says with a smile that would melt most girls' hearts. But I'm immune to his charms because I know how disgusting he can be when he's not trying to impress a girl.

"Mhmm, I know you think I'll do your homework for you, but guess what? I'm busy," I say, trying to keep a straight face.

He looks at me with his big brown eyes, just the way Zorro does when he wants a treat. "Pleeeease," he says with an exaggerated smile. "Coach is mad at me already because I missed practice yesterday."

At almost six feet tall, Nick towers over me, his broad shoulders a stark contrast to my petite frame. I can't help noticing the envy-tinged glances thrown my way by girls passing by on their way to class, and I want to laugh. My relationship with Nick is far from what they probably think it is.

"Fine, I'll do it," I say. "You better come over, and I'll go over the chapter with you. I'm not going to be responsible for you getting kicked off the team if you fail another test."

He gives me a bear hug. "You're the best, Zara."

He bounds off to his first class, while I shove the rest of my stuff into the locker.

"You guys are adorable." I turn to see Priya standing behind me, her dark hair in a thick braid hanging casually over her right shoulder. I envy the way she can make our school uniform look good. On me, the blue-and-black-plaid skirt looks frumpy, but with her long legs, it somehow looks stylish. She's grinning at me now, while simultaneously chewing on a piece of red licorice.

"Ha-ha, you're hilarious," I say, grimacing at her. I snag a piece from the bag she's holding. "You know perfectly well it's not like that with me and Nick."

"Are you sure *Nick* knows that?" she counters, quickening her pace to keep up with me as we walk to class.

"What do you mean? Of *course* he does."

Priya shrugs nonchalantly. "If you say so . . ."

We enter the classroom just in time to slide into our seats before Mr. Adams begins the lesson. I'm sure I have no idea what Priya is talking about. Nick and I know each other almost too well. We are firmly planted in the friend zone. Which is exactly where I want us to be.

CHAPTER THREE

Mr. Adams spends the first half of class discussing the long history of immigration in the US, the majority of it focused only on European immigration in the nineteenth century, leaving out any mention of the more recent waves of immigrants and the injustices they continue to endure. As if the lives and contributions of all those who made this country richer by bringing their traditions and languages and values can be condensed into a single thirty-minute lecture.

It's my turn today to present my US history paper in front of the class. It's worth 30 percent of our final grade, and my stomach is in knots.

I've chosen to write about the inequities and indignities of the US immigration system. Aside from my own personal connection to the topic, it's frustrating to hear all the negative conversations around immigration lately, especially by the white students, most of whom will never know how it feels to leave everything—and everyone—they know behind just for the hope of building a new, better life for themselves and their family. For people of color, this fear is compounded because we know we're not really welcome in a lot of countries. Yet we continue to come from across the world in order to build a better life.

"Zara, are you ready?" Mr. Adams says after he's done telling us about an upcoming test.

I wipe my palms against my skirt as I stand and walk to the front of the class. I'm usually pretty comfortable speaking in public, but today I avoid looking at my classmates as I speak. I try to focus on my words and their importance to me. It's not easy, talking about xenophobic, discriminatory government policies throughout history and how the quotas on immigration always seemed to disproportionately target people of color.

When I finish my presentation, all I want to do is just sit back down, but I know I have to take questions. Maybe no one will care enough to ask me anything. But I'm not so lucky.

Kyra McKintyre raises her hand.

"Umm, I just wanted to say that it's really sad what y'all go through, but I mean, like, why do *we* have to take care of every-one else in the whole world?"

Blood rushes to my face, and for a moment, I don't think I can speak. Then a calm settles over me.

"No one's asking you to take care of anyone. Immigrants do not come here as beggars. They have a lot to offer. They're edu-cated and skilled, so they work just like everyone else. Sometimes they even do the work that *y'all* don't want to do."

I'm surprised to see Kyra blush, which means she actually isn't as ignorant as she sounds.

"What about all the illegals that are flooding our country?" Tyler says. He's sporting his usual arrogant smirk, clearly trying to goad me, but I'm not falling for that. Instead, I pin him with a cold stare.

"Actually, I was talking about *legal* immigration. But since you brought it up, these *illegals*, as you call them, are fleeing from persecution and awful living conditions and they deserve to live in safety just like you. Do you really think anyone would go through what they do if they weren't desperate to save their families?"

Mr. Adams coughs discreetly. "I think we're going a little off-topic here," he says. "Let's stick to relevant questions." He looks around the class. "Anyone have questions about the Immigration Acts of 1917 and 1924?"

• • •

After history, I have biology with Nick, which is good because I'm trying hard not to scream. I meet up with him in the hall-way outside the classroom.

"What's wrong?" he asks.

"Nothing," I lie.

"Are you sure? Because you don't look like nothing's wrong." He scrutinizes my face, his brown eyes dark and intense.

There's really no point in pretending.

"It's just Tyler," I say with a dismissive wave of my hand. "You know what a jerk he is."

"Do you want me to talk to him? I'll see him at football prac-tice later."

I was afraid of this.

"No, Nick," I say in my firmest voice. "I do not want you to talk to him."

The thing is, when it comes to me, Nick can be overprotec-tive. Even though I never act like a damsel in distress, Nick has always seen himself as my knight in shining armor. I've never needed a knight. I can wield my own damn sword when I need to.

"Whatever you say," Nick says as we walk into class. "Just promise me you'll watch out for him."

I squeeze his elbow to let him know that I love him for always having my back.

• • •

I place the last chair in the circle and survey the setup. Nick, Priya, and I are preparing for our Social Justice Club meeting at the recreation center, where a bunch of us meet with Ms. Talbot, my social studies teacher from two years ago, to discuss current events, most of which are the stuff of nightmares, but it helps us understand them better. But we don't just sit around talking about things. Ms. Talbot encourages us to contact our representatives, start petitions, and attend rallies too. She wanted to run these meetings at school, but the administration wouldn't approve it.

Ms. Talbot walks into the room just as we finish setting up the last row of chairs. She's tall and slender and has this energy about her. The kind that inspires you to do great things. Her hair is tied back in a ponytail, and her tortoiseshell glasses make her look more severe than she really is.

"Thank you so much for helping out," she says as she places a large platter of cookies on the desk. "Help yourselves before the horde arrives," she adds with a grin.

Ms. Talbot is my hero. There. I said it. I've had a massive crush on her ever since I took her social studies class sophomore year, and I'm not even the slightest bit embarrassed to admit it. She's totally amazing with all her degrees and accolades and the way she's completely unafraid to say it like it is. Everyone loves her. At least everyone who's a decent human being.

I know she's had to deal with a lot of crap from "concerned" parents, which to me is a synonym for "homophobic" parents. She brings her wife, a human rights lawyer, to school events sometimes, and we've all seen the looks from some of the parents who huddle around, probably worried that their kids are being indoctrinated by their gaydom.

The other students start filing in, and we begin.

"I see some new faces today, so welcome to all of you," Ms. Talbot says, looking around the circle. "Why don't we start by introducing ourselves. Who wants to start?"

A couple of tentative hands go up, and soon everyone is talking, sharing opinions and discussing today's topic, which is the new "License to Discriminate" law. There are many passionate voices here, and it's easy to see why we feel that this is a safe space. Ms. Talbot has a way of making everyone comfortable and encourages the free exchange of ideas. We usually break into smaller groups to brainstorm what we can do. I like it when there are new people, and today there are two in my group. Dylan, who I know from biology but who has never come to one of these meetings until today, and a girl I haven't seen before who told us her name is Chloe. She's slightly taller than me but just as curvy. Her thick brown hair falls in waves around her shoulders, and a silver angel hanging on a braided black cord rests in the hollow of her throat.

"It's Chloe, right?" I say to her. "I don't think I've ever seen you here before?"

She nods. "It's my first time here. I saw a post about it on Instagram."

"What do you think? It's great, right?"

"Yes, I really like Ms. Talbot," she says. "I wish we had a teacher like her at Holy Cross."

I instantly like Chloe, because as far as I'm concerned, anyone who loves Ms. Talbot like I do is cool.

We spend the rest of the meeting talking about an upcoming rally that's taking place in San Antonio this weekend. It's to protest the bills that would put LGBTQ people at further risk for discrimination and abuse. Religious freedom groups have been advocating such laws in order to exercise their rights to turn away same-sex couples from their businesses or to refuse to hire trans people for no reason other than their bigoted beliefs.

This is why our group is so important. We hate the way things are and we want to do something about it. Luckily, we have someone like Ms. Talbot to steer us in the right direction.

CHAPTER FOUR

Chloe stays behind afterward to help put the chairs and tables away.

"I don't know if my parents will let me go to the rally," she tells me as we're putting away the last ones.

"Are you sure? Even if Ms. Talbot talks to them?"

Chloe makes a face. "No way, that's just going to make it worse." She slides a table back to its original position. "They don't even know that I came today. I told them I was going to the library."

"But why wouldn't they want you to be involved?" I say. "I thought parents like extracurricular stuff."

"You haven't met mine," she says, rolling her eyes. "Their idea of extracurriculars is baking cookies for the church bake sale or singing in the church choir. As long as it's something to do with the church." She leans against the table and presses the sides of her head with her fingertips.

I want to comfort her, but I'm not sure what to say. I'm not a religious person. Even though my family is Muslim, it's more in a cultural way than anything else. I don't pray regularly, I fast sporadically during Ramadan, and although I love the traditions and everything, I consider myself an agnostic when it comes to matters of faith. Luckily my parents have always encouraged me to question and explore rather than blindly believe and follow. But I know it's not the same for everyone, Muslim or otherwise.

"Is there anything I can do to help?" I ask tentatively, not wanting to overstep just because she shared something personal.

"Thanks, Zara, but I have to figure this out on my own." She hesitates, then smiles, which doesn't really erase the sadness in her eyes. "I'm sorry, you must think I'm really weird, telling you all this when we've just met. I'm not usually like this."

I shake my head. "It's totally fine. That's what this whole group is about. We get to talk about stuff that we can't talk about anywhere else."

She grabs her bag off the floor and smooths down her skirt. It's a floral pattern, and she's paired it with a light pink top. I can't help noticing that it accentuates the warmth of her brown eyes. I catch myself staring a little too long and quickly look away before she thinks I'm a complete weirdo.

"Anyway . . . thanks for listening," she says. She gives me a little wave as she walks out the door.

I get my stuff and walk out to the parking lot to meet up with Nick and Priya. We're going to Scoopz, the frozen yogurt place where Nick works part-time and gets an employee discount. Priya and I are going to work on our calculus homework, and that requires large amounts of sugar.

"Who was that you were talking to?" Priya asks while she drives us.

"That was Chloe. She goes to Holy Cross."

Nick nods. "I hate those guys. We played them last year, and they're the worst losers."

"Well, Chloe's very nice. But it sounds like she's having problems with her parents."

"What kind of problems?" Nick asks.

"She said they're super religious. Like she wasn't even supposed to be here, so she just lied to them."

"Is she coming to the rally?" Priya asks.

I shrug. "Not sure. Maybe if she can convince her parents. I feel bad for her."

"It's gotta be hard," Priya says. "My parents were kind of worried that I'd get distracted if I joined up, remember?"

"Yeah. It's a good thing you're such a smarty-pants," I say, grinning at her in the rearview mirror.

Priya wants to be a doctor like her father, but she's really interested in medical research, so she plans to apply to a combined MD-PhD program after she graduates from college. I'm pretty ambitious myself, but I can't think quite that far ahead yet.

Once inside Scoopz, we grab a corner table in the back where we can sit for hours without anyone hassling us.

Nick goes into the staff room and reappears wearing an apron and cap. He looks ridiculous—and since this is rare for him, we always make sure to point it out as much as we can when we get a chance.

I top off my raspberry froyo with lots of gummy bears while Priya gets her usual, chocolate mousse.

"You're such an aunty," I tease while trying to snag a spoonful. She holds her cup as far away from me as possible.

"I'm sorry you're still a five-year-old in a seventeen-year-old's body," Priya says, trying to wrestle me off. "Why would you ruin a perfectly good froyo with gummies?"

"You take that back, Priya," I say, waving my spoon around menacingly. Unfortunately, Priya knows all my tricks, and I fail miserably.

"Will you two behave yourselves?" Nick calls out from behind the counter. "There are children here." I turn to give him the finger, but I make sure the kids in question can't see it. Their moms, however, do see me, and I dodge their glares, while Nick calmly serves them with a huge grin on his face.

Priya's wearing her BROWN GIRL MAGIC T-shirt today. It has a picture of a gorgeous, dark-skinned, sari-clad desi girl wearing a bindi as well as a nath, the elaborate nose ring with a gold chain extending all the way to the side of her head, like the ones that Indian brides wear. It's one of my faves because it always gets a lot of shade from random strangers. Priya and I love judging each and every one of them in return. We're petty that way. But eventually we pull out our books and do some actual work. I don't have a lot of time because Ammi's book club is meeting at our place tonight and I want to be done before that.

• • •

Shireen Khala is the first to arrive.

"Assalaam alaikum, Khala."

"Walaikum assalaam, Zara, beta."

She's wearing a beautiful shalwar kameez, lavender with cream-colored flowers embroidered along the neckline and sleeves. She envelops me in a hug, then looks around furtively.

"Where's your ammi?" she whispers, handing me a glass container heavy with her delicious kheer. She knows how much I love it.

"She's in the kitchen," I whisper back. "Why are we whispering?"

"I haven't read the book. Your ammi is going to be so annoyed."

"No, she won't," I lie. "Come in and have some chai. Ammi just made some."

I turn to lead her into the kitchen, but she grabs my arm.

"Wait, Zara, you've read the book, hai na?"

"*The Kite Runner*? Yes, I loved it," I say, my voice rising from excitement.

"Shhhhh." Shireen Khala looks around again. Does she think Ammi's hiding behind the drapes?

"Sorry," I whisper.

"Why don't you quickly tell me what it's about? Then—"

Ammi walks out of the kitchen and saves me from the awkwardness.

"Assalaam alaikum, Shireen. Kaisi ho?" Ammi asks.

Shireen is a couple of years younger and addresses my mom in the traditional way as befits an older sister. "Walaikum assalaam, Nilufer Baji."

After the greetings have been taken care of, Ammi and Shireen Khala adjourn to the living room to have chai while they wait for the others to arrive. I check out the snacks and desserts Ammi has put out on the sideboard. There's her carrot halwa, cut-up mangoes and pineapple, crispy samosas, some spiced cashews, and Shireen Khala's kheer. The creamy rice pudding garnished with golden raisins and pistachios is calling to me, so I spoon some into a bowl and take it to my room.

I'm done with most of my homework, so before long, I'm ready to get into bed. As I fall asleep, a thought weighs on me.

My presentation in class today has reminded me that I exist in a sort of no-man's-land. I wasn't born here, but I don't remember much of Pakistan and I can't imagine what my life would be like if I still lived there. But I know how a lot of people here feel about immigrants.

So . . . where do I belong?

CHAPTER FIVE

The clouds hang low and cast an ominous shadow over the crowds gathered on opposite sides of the street. I find it sort of befitting because this is not a happy occasion. Our group has driven here to San Antonio to join the counterprotest against Bill 235. Ms. Talbot says if this bill passes it will open the door for many other discriminatory laws against groups that are already marginalized. She says it's up to us to push back while we still can. We're all riled up and ready to shout over the angry voices on the other side.

I look at all the people across the street. There are members of a biker gang, various churches, and parent advocacy groups. I wonder who they think they're advocating for. It puzzles me that they would be so worked up about the personal decisions and choices of other people. They carry signs with hateful messages. TURN TO GOD. HE WILL SAVE YOU, one says. A woman carries one that says, STOP TAINTING OUR CHILDREN. A man shouts into a megaphone, and someone on our side picks hers up and starts shouting into it too. Soon no one can hear what the other side is saying. But the hatred is palpable on both sides. Unsuspecting passersby quickly turn around and go back the way they came when they realize what they've stumbled into.

Chloe finishes up her sign and holds it up proudly. JESUS LOVES ALL HIS CHILDREN.

I grin at her. "I'm so glad you made it. We were trying to think of a way to kidnap you if you couldn't get away."

"You have no idea how hard it was to convince them," Chloe says. "Thankfully my grandparents are visiting. Mom and Dad have their hands full."

Just then a chorus erupts from our side, everyone calling out, "Trans rights are human rights!" We join in as the crowd's energy rises, and I can't help feeling lucky that I get to do this. It feels good to shout and drown out the hateful rhetoric coming from the opposite side of the street. It feels good to do something.

• • •

Afterward we all take a stroll along the River Walk and stop to eat dinner. After delicious fish tacos and the best chunky guacamole this side of the Rio Grande, we head back to Corpus. I promised Chloe a ride back to her house, but on impulse we decide to stop at Scoopz for dessert.

It turns out that she's a huge fan of gummy worms as well, and we share a large bowl of mango sorbet topped with sour gummy worms.

"So, are you planning to tell your parents about SJC anytime soon?" I ask once we've settled into a small corner booth. Chloe's wearing a denim jacket with black shorts and a pink top. It brings out a rosiness in her skin, and I realize that her eyes are really more hazel than brown, the golden flecks more noticeable in the sunlight that illuminates our little corner. The angel pendant she wears glints in the light.

"Zara."

I realize that I've been staring at her like an idiot.

"Sorry . . . umm, what were you saying?" I wipe my suddenly sweaty palms against my jeans.

"I was saying that I don't know if I can ever tell them," she says. "I really need this, you know."

She looks away quickly before I can see her eyes water, but not fast enough. I feel an incredible urge to reach across the table and hold her hands, but I'm not sure if I should. Then my hands find their way to hers anyway. She looks at me in surprise, tears falling freely now as we just sit there, the frozen yogurt melting in its bowl between us.

"You know, I don't usually talk about this," she says after a while. She moves her hands away, but only to grab a napkin and blow her nose.

"It's okay. You can talk to me." I play with the plastic spoon, giving her time to compose herself.

"It's just that it's so hard to make them understand," she says. Her eyes are slightly red, the lashes still wet.

"That you want to be part of SJC?"

She shakes her head. "No, it's just everything." She takes a deep breath. "I came out to them last year. And it's been awful."

"Because of church and stuff?"

She nods. "Mostly that. But it's also just how they are. They've always been strict with me, but I really thought they'd understand what I'm going through."

"Maybe they need more time?" I don't know what else to say.

"Maybe. I don't know," she says with a sigh. "At least I don't have to lie anymore. That's a start, I guess."

"It sure is. And maybe when you do tell them about SJC they could come to some of the events."

She gives a little laugh. "I don't think that's ever going to happen."

"You never know," I say. "Maybe if they see how you're trying to change things and make the world a better place, they'll support you."

"That's just it. I've always talked to them about this stuff, but it's like they can't see beyond the church. It's as if that's the only thing they understand."

"I know what you mean. My mom and dad know people like that too. They can't open their minds and see that there are people who are hurting just for wanting to be who they are."

"I know, right? It's so frustrating trying to get through to them. I mean, I'm one of those people and they simply refuse to see it."

Chloe stares down at the bowl between us, and since I don't know what else I can say to make her feel better, I don't say anything while we finish our frozen yogurt. It's a comfortable silence though, and I kind of like this. Being friends with someone who's committed to the same thing as I am, that's important to me, and I'm glad that I can be there for her.

"I'm sorry, I wish I could be more help," I say after our bowls are empty and the sky is turning a deep orange. I take a deep breath. "Hey, do you want to watch a movie later?"

When she doesn't reply right away, I panic.

"Priya invited me and Nick over," I add quickly. "It might get your mind off everything."

She hesitates.

"Are you sure your friends won't mind?" she says.

"Not at all," I say. They better not.

Chloe smiles. "Then yes, I'd love to."

CHAPTER SIX

I text Priya to let her know that I'm bringing Chloe. Priya lives on Ocean Drive in her parents' mansion. As I pull up on their driveway, the front door opens and Priya pops her head out, waving for us to come in. She's wearing one of her signature T-shirts. Tonight, it's a black one that says, YOU'RE THE IDLI TO MY SAMBAR. Underneath the letters is a picture of a platter of steaming rice cakes next to a bowl of spicy lentils.

I grin at her. "Your mom is *the* best."

Chloe looks utterly confused as we step into the cool interior. Gita Aunty, Priya's mom, greets us and ushers us to the dining table. She has to be the most effervescent person I've ever met. She also makes the best South Indian food, and as I cleverly guessed from Priya's T-shirt, she's made idli sambar for us to enjoy before we settle in for the movie. I should have given Chloe a heads-up not to eat beforehand. Gita Aunty would have a conniption if she didn't eat anything. As we dip the steamy, fluffy rice cakes in the spicy lentil-and-vegetable soup, I feel a little sorry for Chloe, who's actually being quite the trouper despite the fact that her face has turned an alarming shade of red. The way I look at it though, the very least that white people can do after colonizing our subcontinent for hundreds of years is appreciate our flavorful cuisine.

Gita Aunty is happily humming along to a Bollywood video playing on the TV. I notice Chloe watching the video in between gulps of ice water.

"You've never watched a Bollywood movie, have you?" Priya asks as we're finishing up.

"I saw one at my friend Tina's house once," Chloe says. "It had subtitles."

"Tina Pereira?" Gita Aunty pipes up from the kitchen, where she's pulling out the idli maker from the pot.

"Yes, do you know her?" Chloe asks.

"Yeah, Mom, do you know her?" Priya echoes with a grin.

It's funny because Priya's mom knows everyone. Or at least everyone who's desi. She works for an NGO and is known for her legendary parties. I'm pretty sure every desi from here to Houston has been to her house at one time or another.

"Of course I know her," Gita Aunty says, placing a platter of freshly steamed idli on the table. Chloe looks a little scared. She's picked up on Gita Aunty's biological imperative to force-feed her guests.

"Is her mom the one who had a nose job?" Priya asks.

"Priya," Gita Aunty says sternly. "We're not supposed to talk about it."

"I knew it," Chloe says under her breath.

Gita Aunty has turned away to ladle more sambar into a bowl.

The three of us grin at one another.

"So, what's the name of this movie you watched with Tina?" I ask.

"*Something and Sons*," Chloe says, biting her lip. "I don't remember, but it'll come to me."

Priya and I exchange a look.

"You mean *Kapoor & Sons*, right?" I say.

"Yes, that's the one," Chloe says. "It was pretty good."

"I'm sorry, excuse me?" Priya stands and puts her hand on her hip. "Pretty good?"

Chloe looks at me in alarm.

"It's okay, Chloe . . . but I'm afraid we can't be friends anymore," I say, appearing perfectly serious.

"Wha—"

"Well, not if you're going to diss Fawad Khan in my presence, young lady," Priya says. Then she breaks into a huge smile at the look of panic on Chloe's face.

"Who's dissing Fawad Khan?" a deep voice says from behind us. We all turn to see Nick standing by the door.

"Ah, Nick, it's nice to see you." Gita Aunty beams at him. "Come and have some idli sambar."

"Thank you, Gita Aunty," Nick says. "And yes, don't mind if I do. I'm starving."

"Are you ever not starving?" I ask him.

"Shut up, Zara," he says, grabbing my plate, but I stop him just in time.

"Oh my God, get your own."

"Children, stop fighting," Priya says as Gita Aunty brings another plate for Nick.

Nick sticks out his tongue at me before turning to dazzle Gita Aunty with a smile. He's such a child.

"So, have we decided what movie to watch?" I ask as we all watch Nick stuff his face.

"I'm up for anything," Priya says unhelpfully.

"Well, good. Then it's decided," I say. "We'll watch ANYTHING. Where's it playing? Somewhere?"

"Ha-ha, you're hilarious," Priya says. "Why don't you just decide as usual?"

"Look, if you could pick for once or Nick could take a break from scarfing down food, maybe I wouldn't have to decide all the time, isn't that right?" I say.

"I thought we were watching a Fawad Khan movie," Nick says, looking up from his plate.

"That's actually a really great idea," Priya says.

"Mhmm." Nick is back to dunking and slurping.

"I'm game if you all are," I say, looking mostly at Chloe, who appears to be a little shell-shocked from all the banter flying around.

"Sure, sounds great to me."

"Okay, then," I say, rubbing my hands gleefully.

Priya puts on *Khoobsurat*. While she and I have always lamented the many Bollywood films in which the female lead is merely eye candy, we have absolutely no problem with a brooding Fawad Khan cast in the same role. His stylish outfits and Mr. Darcy–like demeanor have us all but drooling on our popcorn. Chloe's eyes are glued to the screen every single time he appears in a scene, and Priya and I have resorted to throwing popcorn at her hair to prove how oblivious she is to everything else in that moment.

Halfway through the movie, Nick sighs dramatically. He's already seen this movie twice at my house. He gets up to grab some water in the kitchen and discreetly waves at me to come to him.

"Are you gonna watch the whole thing?" he whispers to me as I grab a glass from the cabinet.

"Um, yes, that's generally how it works," I say.

"Fine, it's just that . . . I thought it was only going to be the three of us."

"Chloe's going through a really hard time," I say softly. "What do you want me to do?"

Nick makes a face, and we go back to the living room to finish watching the movie.

• • •

I think Chloe has a good time . . . but it's hard to tell. She says all the right things when we say goodbye to Priya and Nick, but I can also sense there's something else underneath.

We talk a little about the movie as I drive her home. It's not until I'm dropping her off in front of her house that she turns to me and says, "Hey, I hope I didn't mess up your plans for tonight."

"No, not at all," I answer quickly. "It was fun."

"I just thought that Nick didn't seem too happy." She tucks a strand of her hair behind her ear and looks at me, her ridiculously long eyelashes casting a shadow on her cheeks.

"Don't worry about it. He was just being a brat," I say.

"Can I ask you something?"

"Sure, what is it?"

"Are you two together or . . . ?" Her voice trails off as if she realizes that maybe she shouldn't be asking.

"No, no—we're just friends," I say quickly. Very quickly. "We've known each other since we were five and hang out together a lot."

"Oh, okay." She studies her hands, and it feels like she's going to say something else.

But then a light goes on inside her house, and she stiffens.

"I have to go," she says, grabbing her bag. "Hey, thanks for the ride and the movie and . . . everything." She opens the door and climbs out of the car.

"Anytime!" I call out. She gives a quick little wave and walks away. I wait until she's inside before driving home.

Later, as I'm getting ready for bed, I can't help wondering why she asked about me and Nick. I drift off to sleep with a picture of her beautiful brown eyes looking into mine.

CHAPTER SEVEN

"Priya's waiting for us. You ready for lunch?" I ask Nick as we walk out of English class together the next day. It's a nice day, not too muggy, so we start walking over to the baseball field. Tyler passes us on the way. I'm with Nick, so my stomach doesn't churn as it usually does. But then Tyler makes an exploding motion with his hands just as we're passing by, and I push down the urge to punch him in the throat. Nick, on the other hand, has no such reservations. He steps toward Tyler, menacing and ready to fight.

"Nick, don't." I grab his right arm and pull him back. "It's not worth it."

"Yeah, Garcia," Tyler taunts. "Better listen to your girlfriend. Otherwise, you know—"

Nick lunges again, and I tighten my grip to keep him back.

Thankfully, Tyler walks away, and I release the breath I've been holding. Nick jerks his arm out of my reach and glares at me.

"Why did you stop me, Zara?" He's breathing hard, and I can feel the anger coming off him in waves.

"Because I don't want any trouble."

"But why should he get away with it every single time?"

"Look," I say forcefully, "I don't need you to step in for me all the time. I can take care of myself."

"I know you can, but . . . he's such a jerk." His eyes are still dark with anger.

"He's not worth it, Nick," I say, my tone gentler now, because I know exactly how he feels.

We keep on walking and join Priya, who's already in our usual spot. Nick unwraps his lunch and looks over at me. We swap our lunches wordlessly while Priya watches with a bemused expression on her face.

"You two are so weird," she says.

"What? I don't feel like chutney sandwiches today," I say. "And Nick has pizza."

"Zawash mom maksh zha besh sad wishes," Nick says.

"Huh?" Priya stares at him blankly.

I'm immensely grateful that Nick finishes chewing and swallows before speaking again.

"I was just saying that Zara's mom makes the best sandwiches," he says.

I grin at him, take a bite of my pizza, and wave my slice in the air.

"Thanks, dude. Jalapeños and onions. You know me so well."

He throws a pack of gum my way. "You're gonna need that."

• • •

"Zara, Nick, come down. Dinner is ready!" Ammi calls up from the kitchen, and we hurry down because today is chicken quorma night and we're starving. Nick came over so I could help him with chem and of course he's invited himself to stay for dinner.

"How were the chutney sandwiches today, Nick?" Ammi asks innocently. Sometimes I could swear that she actually makes them more for Nick than for me.

"Really good, Aunty," Nick replies. "And the quorma smells amazing." He grabs the plate of hot, buttery naan Ammi is holding out and carries it to the table. Abbu walks into the kitchen, sniffs the air appreciatively, and brings the steaming serving dish over.

"Hi, Uncle," Nick says.

Abbu pats Nick on the shoulder. "You haven't been over for dinner for some time, Nick."

"It's been four days, Abbu. Calm down," I say with a grin. Abbu loves it when Nick is over because then he has someone to watch and talk football with. Ammi grabs the salad, and we can finally dig in.

"So how was school?" Abbu asks, tearing off a piece of naan and dunking it in the gravy.

"It's okay, just the usual," I say.

I can feel Nick's eyes burning a hole in my skull, but I ignore him, choosing instead to focus on the deliciousness in my mouth.

"How are things with that boy?" Ammi asks. "Has he been bothering you anymore?"

Nick makes a weird noise, and I swear to God he'd better be choking because if he says a word about what happened I'm going to shove a giant piece of naan down his throat.

"Are you okay there, Nick?" Abbu asks, handing him a glass of water.

"I'm fine," Nick says brightly. "It's just Tyler—"

I kick him hard under the table.

"Ouch. What was that for?"

Oh my God. He's such an idiot.

I quickly take a gulp of water and swallow it very slowly. Everyone is looking at me strangely.

"It's nothing, I'm fine," I say reassuringly.

They're not buying it. Nick will pay for this later.

"Zara, beta, please tell us if something is going on," Ammi says, her face already worried. This is exactly what I've been trying to avoid.

"Ammi, Tyler's just being stupid. Right, Nick?" I look pointedly at him.

Nick stares back at me, defiantly chewing his food, and says nothing.

Great. *Now* he decides to stay quiet.

"Nick, do you have something you'd like to share with us?" Abbu asks.

"Tyler did something again today," Nick says quietly. He avoids looking directly at me.

"Did what exactly?" Abbu says, still calm. It takes a lot to get him riled up.

"He just always makes these, you know, racist comments, and then today he did this—"

He makes the exploding gesture, and Abbu's face darkens.

"I'm going to talk to your principal and sit down with this boy and his parents," Abbu says. "Until then, you be careful."

CHAPTER EIGHT

Soon it's the weekend, and I'm heading to the library to study for my chem test. I'm not too thrilled about the fact that Abbu and Nick have taken over the living room and are watching the game. Between their yelling at the TV every few minutes and Ammi's obsession with her new Ninja blender, I can't hear myself think, so I've exiled myself. The sun is blazing hot as usual and it's a relief to enter the cool interior of the library. I look for a quiet spot, and I'm making a beeline for one in the far corner by the bay window when I spot Chloe sitting in one of the study carrels.

I sneak up behind her and tap her on the shoulder. She jumps and screams, earning me a glare from the person beside her. He smugly points at the big sign with bold letters that proclaims this area to be for quiet study. *Calm down, dude.*

"What are you doing here?" Chloe whispers as I put my stuff down on the table to her right. The big Z charm on my purse makes a loud clanging sound, and Mr. Stick-Up-His-Ass sighs dramatically.

Chloe throws him an apologetic smile and glares at me.

36

"I can't study at home," I tell her. "Football."

She nods. "Do you usually come here to study?"

"No, not really. I need to be in my own space."

She looks at my books. "I come here all the time. This is my usual spot."

"Cool." I'm not sure why I can't think of anything else to say. I just stand there like a complete idiot.

"So, chem, huh? Me too. I have a test coming up."

"Same. Acids and bases?"

"Yeah," she says. "I guess we're on pretty much the same timeline."

"Do you want to study together?" I blurt out before I can stop myself. The truth is that I've been thinking about her a great deal.

We move to another section to be away from Grumpy Guy.

"I'm having a really hard time understanding titrations," Chloe says after we've been working on problems for a while.

"Well, lucky for you, I'm here," I say with a grin. I'm glad Nick isn't here right now because he would be rolling his eyes at my dorky attempt at flirting. I know that I have absolutely no game, but this is the best I can do.

I work through a couple of questions with her, and then she's good for the rest. A couple of hours later, she puts down her pen and stretches. I look up, and she smiles at me.

"Hey, thanks for helping me understand this stuff," she says. "I really can't afford to do badly on this test."

"I'm sure you'll do great," I say. I reach over and squeeze her hand gently. "Don't worry so much."

"I just really need to get away from here, you know," she says. "For college."

"Have you thought about where you want to go?"

"As far away from here as possible," she answers without hesitation. "Just someplace where I can breathe."

"Things are still pretty bad at home?" My hand is still on top of hers, and she doesn't move it away or anything.

"You know what?" she says suddenly. "Let's take a break and get frozen yogurt."

"Sounds great to me. Scoopz?" I ask hopefully.

"Of course. Where else?"

Fifteen minutes later, we're sitting in a corner booth with our bowls in front of us. Once again, we go for sour gummies.

"I feel like we're soul mates," I say as I pop a couple of red gummies in my mouth.

I'm kind of glad that Nick isn't working today because I'm not sure what this is yet, but I know it's something. Chloe is a lot more reserved than I am—or at least that's the impression I've gotten. I don't want to scare her away by being too much. And if Nick were here, he'd be making weird faces and smooching noises like the brat he is. Solo, I might be able to play it cool.

"I've never had a soul mate before," she says, looking off into the distance. I almost choke on a piece of the sour gummy.

"Yeah . . . me neither . . ." I say between coughs as I try to clear my airway. "But right now, this froyo can be both of our soul mates."

Real smooth, Zara. Real smooth.

"Oh, okay," she says, her face completely unreadable.

I don't know what to say next because a thousand questions are tumbling around in my useless brain right now.

She starts talking about some TV show that she really likes, and I promise to check it out. I'm glad the awkward moment is over . . . and I'm sad when she suggests going back to the library.

• • •

That evening, there's a news story about a terrorist attack that killed four Americans in Pakistan. The next day, I dodge dirty looks from everyone. I swear they think I'm some sort of mastermind who single-handedly controls the entire Muslim ummah. It's always the same. I'm exhausted from the burden of representing almost two billion people. It's gotten to the point where anytime there's a crime reported in the news, I find myself praying that the perpetrator is white and non-Muslim.

After SJC that afternoon, Ms. Talbot pulls me aside. "Are you okay?" she asks, her eyes filled with concern. "You were awfully quiet today."

"It's nothing new," I say. "Did you hear about the attack on the US embassy in Islamabad yesterday?"

"I did. It's awful," she says. "Did someone say something?"

She's very astute, but it doesn't surprise me. It makes it easy for me to talk to her because I don't have to explain every little thing to her. There aren't a lot of people here that I can talk to without it taking a lot out of me.

"Not really to me, but I can tell what they're thinking," I say. "Sometimes I wonder if I'm imagining it all."

"Probably not," Ms. Talbot says. "Most people won't take the time to educate themselves about issues that affect us all. It's easy to think that a lot of it is happening so far away that we don't need to bother."

"I guess, but then why do I feel guilty every time something like this happens? I mean, I'm not remotely responsible in any way, but it feels like I'm supposed to take the blame."

"Zara, of course you don't have to do anything like that," Ms. Talbot says. She leans against the table and looks at me. "Please don't ever think that. I'm so proud of what you're doing here. This is what matters, making people aware. But it's going to take time."

"I know," I say with a deep sigh. "But it's so frustrating."

"Hang in there," she says. "And remember I'm always here for you."

• • •

My heavy heart lifts a little when I see that Chloe's waiting for me. We walk out to our cars together.

"I couldn't help overhearing what you two were talking about," she says. "I'm so sorry."

"I'm fine," I say. "Just tired of the same old thing, I guess."

"I know it's not the same thing," Chloe says, "but I get being tired of all the ignorance. My parents make me go to these church events, and sometimes I just want to scream at their conversations."

"You mean about queer people?"

"Oh my God, Zara, you can't even imagine how ridiculous they sound. It's like they've been living under a rock."

"Sadly, I can imagine. I know people like that too. They talk about us like we're a different species altogether."

We reach my car, and she suddenly turns to face me.

"Hey, let's do something fun. I wanna cheer you up." Her face is so earnest, I can't say no.

It turns out that we both love Marvel movies. When Chloe asks me if I want to see the latest one with her, I don't tell her I've already seen it with Nick. I love Marvel enough to watch the movies multiple times, and I can't wait to be alone in a dark movie theater with Chloe. The possibilities are endless. Maybe I'll casually put my hand on her armrest and see if anything happens. I'm not expecting any Bollywood-type action, but a little hand-holding would go a long way in helping me figure out if Chloe feels anything at all beyond friendship.

We drop my car off at my house, and I run in to tell my parents that I'm going to the movies. Soon enough, Chloe and I are seated in the luxury loungers in one of the Century 16 theaters on South Padre Island Drive. Chloe puts her drink in the cup holder between us, so it looks like any hand shenanigans are out of the question. But then the lights dim, and I notice her moving her cup to the other side, and I start to get a little sweaty. I don't know what this says about my social skills, but I made peace with my awkwardness a long time ago. I take a deep, shaky breath and casually let my hand fall somewhere in the middle of the armrest. I know it would be weird to turn my head in her direction to see if she's noticed. So I resist the urge. For about two minutes. She turns her head slightly, and I look away quickly, pretending to be engrossed by the movie trailer on the screen. But then I feel her slide her hand into mine, and everything feels right. I curl my fingers around hers, and we watch the movie.

My heart is beating a million miles per second, and I have the urge to burst into song. Something romantic and cheesy from a Shah Rukh Khan movie.

Even when the movie's over, I don't want the evening to end just yet, so I suggest we get milkshakes.

"Should we just share one?" Chloe asks when we're standing in line at La Paletera.

"Sure, that sounds good. You pick though."

Chloe orders a cookies-and-cream milkshake, and we find a table in the back.

"So, did you love the movie or what?" Chloe asks, sliding the glass toward me. I take a slow pull of my straw, trying to calm my nerves.

We both reach for the glass at the same time, and our fingers touch. Hers are on top of mine, and she just keeps them there. Our eyes meet and linger for the first time during this whole evening. A wave of longing washes over me, and I want nothing more than to lean over and kiss her lips. To taste the strawberry-vanilla lip gloss that I imagine she's wearing. But I can't forget where I am. Here in Corpus we're still a little behind the times.

Chloe just smiles, and I wish I could read her mind. Is she as nervous as I am?

We talk about the movie, but it's what we don't say that has me all tingly inside. We pass the milkshake back and forth, and every time our fingers touch I feel a charge running through me. It's like a spark has been lit and a slow fire is burning inside. I don't want the milkshake to finish, so we can keep doing this. But I also need it to be done so we can move on to the next part.

Chloe takes a long, long sip, a smile in her eyes as she holds my gaze.

Maybe I'm not the only one who feels this way.

"Ready to go?" she asks when we've finished every last drop of the milkshake.

We walk out into the sultry evening. Her car is parked a few short steps away, and we get in. I turn slightly to buckle in my seat belt, and she reaches out to cup my cheek at the exact same moment. That's all the encouragement I need. I lean in, and when our lips touch, something delicious and warm flows through me. Chloe's lips move tentatively on mine, and it's so sweet because it says everything perfectly. Also, I was right—she *does* taste of vanilla and strawberry.

We stop kissing, and somehow our hands find each other. We sit in a comfortable silence for a few seconds.

"So, this happened," Chloe says, and I can hear the smile in her voice.

"Well, I was hoping it would. I mean, you don't just share a milkshake with a girl and then leave her hanging." I cringe as soon as the words come out. What does that even mean?

"You know I've been working up the nerve since the first time we talked," Chloe says.

"I'm glad you finally did," I say as we lean into each other again.

I want to stay with her in this bubble of happiness for as long as we can.

CHAPTER NINE

Hey. Is it okay if I come over?

It's Nick. For the past few days, I've been blowing him off to spend time with Chloe, and I feel guilty.

I'm taking the dogs for a walk.

I'll come with you. Just gimme a sec.

Sure. Chloe's here too.

A few seconds go by.

Actually, I just remembered, I have to take Abuela to the senior center.

Is he for real?

Sure. Whatever.

Chloe and I head out to Ocean Drive with Zorro and my elderly neighbor's dogs, Lola and Felix. I walk them for her sometimes when she's not feeling too great. The sun is setting, and there's a slight breeze that makes it bearable to be outside. The mosquito repellent I sprayed on myself is sticky, but I prefer not to be eaten alive by mosquitoes. Chloe opted against any spray. I promise to make sure her tombstone says she's a hero.

Zorro flirts with Lola the entire way, and Felix is not having any of it. After getting tangled up in their leashes multiple times and almost falling over a kid on a tricycle, I decide that Chloe can hold Zorro. He behaves better if he's with someone else. Felix calms down, and Lola is completely oblivious to the chaos she's causing. After we've walked for a while and the dogs start getting tired, we give them a drink and sit on one of the benches by the water. It's a beautiful evening, marred only by the buzzing mosquitoes that are eating Chloe alive.

"I wanted to ask you something," Chloe says. In reply, I smack her on the thigh.

"Ouch." She glares at me, but I point triumphantly at the mosquito carcass on her leg. She flicks it away. "*Anyway*, I was wondering about something. Do your parents know?"

"That I'm bisexual? Yeah, I told them last year."

"And they were okay with it?" Chloe is barely able to hide her shock.

"Well, yeah, they were surprised at first and a little worried, but we talked about it and then they were okay."

We stare out at the water. The light of the setting sun makes it look as if it's on fire.

Chloe sighs. "I wish my parents had taken it as well as yours."

A wave of sadness washes over me. "I'm sure they just need

time to get used to the idea." I take her hand in mine and squeeze gently.

"It's not that. They just don't accept it. I told you, they're super religious and this goes against all their beliefs."

"I can't imagine how difficult it must be for you," I say, wanting to comfort her in some way. "I have a friend in Houston who's Muslim like me, and he's having a really tough time with his parents too."

"I just wish they would stop trying to make me feel so guilty all the time. I mean, I love them, but this is so messed up." She looks at me, and her eyes are full of tears. My heart breaks for her.

"You know I'm always here for you, right?"

She leans into me, and we sit just like this for a bit. The dogs start getting restless, so we drop them off and head over to my house.

"Why don't you come in and meet my parents?" I offer. I don't want her to have to go home feeling the way she is.

She nods, and we head inside. Ammi is already there making dinner.

"Ammi, this is my friend Chloe. Chloe, this is my mom."

"Hi, Chloe. Would you like to stay for dinner? I'm almost done," Ammi says. "It's just egg curry and roti. Do you like Pakistani food?"

"Is it like Indian food? I *love* naan bread," Chloe says. I cringe at her use of the term *naan bread*. I've stopped trying to explain to people that naan is a type of bread, so you can just call it naan. Otherwise it's like saying *bun bread* or *roll bread*.

I decide now is not the time to correct her. Instead, I say, "So, you'll stay?" And I'm genuinely excited when she says yes.

Abbu comes home soon after, and we all eat dinner together. I look at Chloe as she chats with Abbu, and she looks so happy and comfortable. It's important to me that my parents and my girlfriend like each other. Girlfriend. Hmm. I wonder if that's what she is to me. We haven't really talked about anything like that yet.

"Zara, you never told me you like to sing." Chloe's voice pulls my attention back to the conversation.

"What? Oh, just karaoke," I say hurriedly before this becomes a thing. "Actually, my dad is really good, right, Abbu?"

Abbu smiles.

"No, no, nothing like that," he says, waving dismissively. "When I was much younger, I used to sing ghazals sometimes. Now I just like to sing along to Bollywood songs."

"C'mon, Abbu, don't be so modest. You know you're much better than that," I say.

Chloe smiles at Abbu. "I'd love to hear you sing something."

I'd love to kiss her on the lips right now, but I restrain myself.

"Zara, why don't you set up the karaoke machine?" Ammi says. She doesn't have to ask me twice. I go to the living room and set everything up. Abbu bought the karaoke machine as a gift for the whole family at Christmas when I was ten. We still pull it out every now and then, especially when the desi aunties and uncles come over. Then it's practically a Bollywood festival.

I look through our stack of karaoke CDs until I find one that Abbu brought back from Pakistan a few years ago. Mohammed Rafi and Lata Mangeshkar, my favorite Bollywood singers. When it comes to Hindi music, I'm partial to the oldies.

"Abbu, please can you sing 'Khoya Khoya Chand'?" I beg, and Abbu smiles. It's one of his faves too. As the music starts and he begins to sing, I lean back with Chloe next to me. Ammi shoots us a look, and I wonder if she can tell how I feel about Chloe.

"He's so good," Chloe whispers in my ear. "I don't understand a word of it, but it's beautiful."

"I'll tell you what it means later," I whisper back. I feel content in this moment, sitting here with this girl I really like, listening to Abbu sing. She fits in perfectly somehow. I mean, she's just met them, and I love how comfortable she is already. I'm careful not to let my parents notice, but I slide my hand into hers under one of the mirrorwork pillows that Ammi brought back from Pakistan.

Later, when Chloe is ready to leave, I walk her out to her car.

"So, do you want me to tell you what the song was all about?" I ask, shamelessly batting my eyelashes at her. I pull out all the stops when I really want something, and this is the best flirting technique I know. Maybe I should study Bollywood movies more carefully.

"Sure. I'd love to hear it. Are you going to sing it to me?" she says, laughter bubbling up in her eyes.

"No, no, I just think you should know what you listened to, that's all," I say quickly.

Chloe leans against the side of her car while I strike what I hope is a dramatic Bollywood-style pose à la Sharmila Tagore and begin.

"Oh, bashful moon in the vast sky,
Your eyes will see the night pass.

How will you sleep?
Oh, bashful moon,
The intoxicating wind blows,
The flower in my heart blossoms
My soul quivers."

Chloe's lips drown out the rest of my words. Somewhere in the back of my mind a small voice reminds me that Ammi and Abbu are just inside, but that only seems to make this kiss more intoxicating.

"Zara, do you have any idea how much I like you?" Chloe says, leaning back.

"No, but I'd love to know," I say, suddenly feeling very self-conscious.

"But is it okay if I don't have a song?" she teases. Then she adds softly, "Do you really need me to tell you?"

I shake my head. I can see it in her eyes. I can tell by the way her body gravitates toward mine when we're standing close. I know we haven't spent that much time together, but sometimes you just know. At least I know I do. I feel a connection—a connection that grew even stronger tonight when she was in my home with my family.

My parents love me unconditionally, even when I put them in difficult situations. They only care about my happiness, not what society tells them they should care about. And I respect them so much for it. I have friends who struggle with who they are because their families don't accept them. I know I'm one of the lucky ones. I could never really be with someone they didn't love too. And I know they will love Chloe.

"Hey, where'd you go?" Chloe swings my hand back and forth gently. "Are you okay?"

She looks worried suddenly, and I realize it's because she thinks she's pushing too soon.

"Yes, I'm okay," I say, pulling her head closer to mine and kissing her softly on the lips. "Chloe, you know whenever you feel that things are getting too hard for you with your parents . . . you can always come here." I put my arms around her.

In the moonlight, her eyes shine brightly. "Thank you," she whispers in my ear.

She gets in her car and drives off. I stand there until I can no longer see her before turning to go back inside. Ammi is just starting the dishwasher when I come in.

"I like Chloe," she announces, wiping her hand on a kitchen towel. She comes closer and gently touches my face. "You really like her, don't you, chanda?"

My cheeks are on fire as I nod.

She laughs. "Achha, now you're acting all shy. But for chumma-chummi in front of the house, you're not too shy."

"Oh my God, Ammi, stop," I say, worried that Abbu will hear.

"It's okay, beta," Ammi says teasingly. "You don't have to tell me anything if you don't want to."

"There's nothing to tell, Ammi," I say, taking the large serving bowl she's holding out and putting it in the cabinet.

"Let me tell you," she begins, "when your abbu and I first realized how we felt about each other, we had to keep it a secret from everyone."

My parents' love story has always felt like a romance novel to me. Star-crossed lovers from different social classes, fighting with the whole world to be together. And even though I've heard the story so many times, I never grow tired of listening.

"You know when my father found out about Abbu, he threatened to kick me out of the house." Ammi's eyes glisten a little. My grandfather passed away a few years ago. After all the drama about my parents' marriage, he was the one who was closest to me of all our extended family in Pakistan.

"I wish Nana was still here," I say. "Remember how he taught me to play carrom?"

Ammi nods mournfully. She hadn't seen him for years and didn't get to go when he was dying.

"Ammi, don't be sad. Isn't it good that he was happy for you after all?"

"I just wish he could see you so grown-up," she says wistfully. "He would be very proud."

"At least Nani will get to see us soon."

I love visiting Pakistan. I've only been twice since I was a baby, but each time it was like getting a giant hug. I was spoiled and pampered, and it was wonderful.

"Hopefully we'll get called for our green card interview soon," Ammi says. "Once we have those, we won't have to worry about going back and forth to Karachi."

"Are you worried about Nani?"

"She's not doing so well, and your dada and dadi are also getting older. We may not have too many years left. I'd like us to go and see them soon."

"It'll be fine, Ammi."

The hospital where Abbu works is sponsoring him, and the lawyers have told him our application for permanent residence is at the last stage and that we won't have to wait much longer. It'll be a huge relief for all of us once we have green cards. With things the way they are, there's always this fear hanging over us that something will happen to mess up the process. It's no way to live.

To distract Ammi, I suggest watching another episode of *Zindagi Gulzar Hai*. We've been watching the TV drama for a while now, but lately it's been hard finding the time.

Fawad Khan is totally worth staying up late for.

CHAPTER TEN

A few days later, I'm standing in the principal's office, my stomach all twisted up in a knot. Abbu didn't waste any time calling for a meeting with Tyler and his dad, but the principal took his time setting it up. Now there's only one problem: Tyler's dad isn't here.

I wish I could say I'm surprised, but I'm not. I do, however, regret telling Abbu anything, because I knew this would happen. Now Abbu is going to go all Amrish Puri on the principal, and I have a bad feeling that this will not end well. Because this is not a Bollywood movie and Abbu is not a villain.

Our principal, Mr. Trevino, is bent over some forms, probably the incident report for today's meeting. He looks up over his reading glasses, which sit halfway down his nose.

"We were expecting to see your father here as well." Mr. Trevino addresses Tyler, who is sitting in one of the four chairs arranged in a semicircle on the other side of the desk.

Tyler shrugs. "Something came up," he says nonchalantly, not bothering to look at any of us.

"Dr. Hossain, would you like to reschedule this meeting for another day?" Mr. Trevino asks.

My father is usually a pretty mild-mannered individual, but I can tell that he is as furious as I am. Tyler's dad not showing up is a blatant show of disrespect toward us that Tyler isn't even trying to hide. I can see a vein throbbing at Abbu's temple.

"No, Mr. Trevino, I don't want to reschedule," Abbu says. "I think it's clear that Mr. Benson doesn't think this is a serious issue at all."

"I assure you that the school is taking this very seriously, Dr. Hossain. Our students' safety is a priority here."

His words ring hollow and rehearsed. I would find him more believable if he just told us that Tyler's dad was too big a donor to the school to warrant any real consequences for his son.

I can tell that Abbu is thinking the same thing. He stands to leave, then pauses. I hold my breath.

"Mr. Trevino, I send my daughter to your school to get a good education," he says. "I expect that you will do everything you need to do to make sure that this kind of behavior is not repeated."

Abbu then looks pointedly at Tyler—and I can't believe it, but it looks like Tyler is squirming under his glare.

"This will not happen again," Abbu pronounces.

That's it.

End of meeting.

• • •

The ride home is uncomfortably silent. I dread facing Tyler at school tomorrow. He might have squirmed for a moment, but I have no doubt that right now he's making fun of us to his friends.

Ammi has dinner waiting for us when we get home.

"So, what happened? Are they going to do anything about this boy?" Ammi spoons portions of murgh cholay on two plates and sets them on the table.

"Nilufer, I don't think they will be able to do anything," Abbu says, washing his hands at the sink and wiping them dry. "That principal seems quite useless."

"So, then what are we going to do about it?" Ammi flips the last roti and brings an entire batch to the table.

"Honestly, Ammi," I say, "I don't know. Tyler's dad is very connected, and Tyler is on the football team. I really don't think he's going to get in trouble for this. I'll just have to deal with him."

Ammi scowls at Abbu. "Iqbal, what is this? I thought you were going to take care of things."

Abbu frowns and slams his fist on the table. Ammi and I both flinch as the dishes clatter. Abbu's face is dark with anger.

"What do you want me to do, Nilufer? Do you think I should have punched that arrogant boy in the face?" Even though I know his anger is not directed at us, I'm still shocked that he's raised his voice at Ammi.

Ammi's eyes widen for a moment before softening. She puts her hand gently on his shoulder.

"Iqbal, of course I don't want you to do anything like that. But we have to do something to stop this, hai na?"

"Haan, Nilufer, lekin main kya karoon? What can I do? I have to be careful that I don't make things worse for Zara."

My stomach is in knots. Despite Abbu's height and glowering, mustachioed appearance, he's just a big softie on the inside. The patients in his pediatric practice love him, as do their parents. There's just something so comforting about him that children gravitate toward. But none of that changes the fact that, to people like Tyler and his dad, my father is nothing but a Muslim immigrant, always "the other."

I know that feeling well. It's a sense of encroachment on someone else's space, an *unbelonging* that never goes away, no matter what you do to fit in. And although I love my life here, it takes just one person like Tyler to make me feel I can never fully belong. I don't want to believe that the color of my skin, my beliefs, and my native tongue will forever brand me an outsider, but Tyler makes that seem like a real possibility.

"Zara, maybe it's best to lie low and let the administration do their job," Abbu says. "Hopefully, Tyler will stop, now that we've formally complained."

Ammi nods. "You know, beta, our green card process is still going on and who knows how long that will take. The way things are these days, we don't want to draw attention to ourselves."

After all these years, they still have no peace of mind when it comes to their lives here.

"Don't worry, Ammi," I say in what I hope is a reassuring tone. "It'll be fine. Now that Mr. Trevino is aware of all this, I'm sure Tyler will back off."

"Yes," Abbu says, leaning over to rub Ammi's shoulder. "Don't worry too much, Nilufer. It will all be okay."

"I'm going to go do my homework," I say, picking up my plate and carrying it to the sink. "Do you want me to do the dishes?"

"Nahin chanda, you go and study," Ammi says.

Abbu's already clearing up. "I'll do the dishes. Nilufer, why don't you go and put on that new Fawad Khan movie? I'll join you as soon as I'm done here."

Back in my room, my mind swirls with the thoughts I can't say out loud to my parents. The worry about our immigration status always sits just below the surface, tarnishing everything good in our lives. We try to remember that our lives are so much better than many others and we are grateful, but it's hard sometimes, always waiting for the other shoe to drop.

My father is a pediatrician, and that affords us certain

luxuries. I go to an expensive private school and hope to go to an Ivy League school after I graduate. But beneath all that positivity is the shadow of still being on an immigrant status. It means everything can be taken away from us. Anger surges through me at the thought that it may only take one phone call from Tyler's dad to Homeland Security to put us all at risk of being deported.

I try to shake off the frustration of knowing that I have to be the one to back off when it's Tyler who's being a racist jerk. Right now, the only thing I can do is focus on school and hope that we get our green cards soon. It's been eight years since we applied, and it's taking a toll on us all.

CHAPTER ELEVEN

Priya and I are eating lunch together in our usual spot under the trees on the edge of the baseball field. Nick's away for a game again, so it's just the two of us and I'm glad because I need to vent.

"Why is Nick being such a brat lately?" I ask.

"What do you mean? What's he doing?" Priya asks. She tears open a bag of chips and holds it out to me.

I'm on my period and jalapeño chips are my staple. Well, technically they're my staple all the time, but especially today. My lunch consists of a bag of sour gummies, a Mars bar, and Priya's chips.

"He's being so weird," I say. "Ever since that night we watched *Khoobsurat* at your place."

"Weird how?" Priya says. She grabs a handful of sour gummies and pops a couple in her mouth.

"I don't know. I think he's just sulking because I'm spending so much time with Chloe." I let out a big sigh.

"I like Chloe," Priya says. She picks out all the green gummies and gives them to me. "Are you sure Nick doesn't have feelings for you? Because it sounds to me like he's jealous."

I hold my head in my hands. "I swear I'm going to get *Nick and I are just friends* tattooed on my forehead."

"Wait, what . . . you're getting a tattoo," Priya says, her eyes wide. "And your parents are letting you? They're so cool."

"Shut up. You know what I mean," I say, snatching the bag of chips from her hands. "Just for that, I'm finishing the rest of these."

● ● ●

This week at SJC we're planning to go to Victoria to show support to a Muslim community organization there that's holding an event to combat Islamophobia and stand together against terrorism and hate. Predictably, right-wing groups began filing complaints and protesting the event as soon as it was announced.

"So, it looks like a local patriot group has created an event on Facebook," I tell the group at the meeting. "They're planning to hold a rally on Saturday, right on the school grounds."

"At least they won't be able to bring guns," Chloe says. "Unless they're willing to break the law and bring weapons onto school property."

"Somehow I doubt that they're terribly concerned with the law," Ms. Talbot says, her tone sarcastic but her face showing concern.

"I read the comments," Meghan says. "They're saying someone should bring a pig. It's ridiculous. I mean, I know Muslims don't eat pork, but what do they think will happen if they bring one to the rally?"

Meghan's from my school and has traveled around a lot with her parents and hates how things are just like I do.

"Maybe they think all of us will spontaneously combust at the mere sight of a pig," I say with a sigh. "I don't know what to think anymore."

"Do we have a plan in case things get out of control?" Jake asks. He's a student from another school but has been coming here since the beginning of the semester.

"Well, the event organizers have said we'll be behind the fence," Ms. Talbot says. "But at the first sign of trouble, we're to go into the building. Plus, I've been told that there's going to be a lot of security."

After the meeting, Chloe and I stay behind to help break down chairs. It's become sort of a routine now, and I like having this time with her.

We're just sharing our love for *The Good Place*, when the door opens and a woman's head appears.

"Melissa, are you just about ready to go?"

Ms. Talbot, who's just writing something in her thick SJC binder, looks up.

"Sylvia . . . I'm so sorry, I lost track of time," she says, waving the woman in. "Come in. You have to meet the girls."

The woman walks in, her high heels clicking on the tile floor. She's wearing a dark gray blazer and pants paired with a light pink blouse. Her dark hair is tied in a knot at the nape of her neck. She approaches Ms. Talbot and pecks her delicately on the cheek.

"Girls, this is my wife, Sylvia. You may have seen her at the open house. Sylvia, this is Zara and Chloe. They've been kind enough to clean up after meetings."

We exchange greetings and then resume cleaning up while Ms. Talbot and her wife talk softly by her desk. I catch Chloe throwing glances in their direction and wonder if she's thinking what I'm thinking: That the two of them are the coolest couple and so cute together.

Later Chloe and I go for froyo again, which is becoming

another one of our routines. It's a weeknight and I have home-work to finish, but I don't get to see Chloe that much outside of SJC these days. Her parents have been all over her for going out too often, so it's been hard for us to spend much time together.

"How cute are Ms. Talbot and her wife?" Chloe says as soon as we slide into our usual booth at Scoopz. She's convinced me to try the caramel pretzel, and I have to admit that it's really good.

"So adorable," I say, my mouth full of caramel goodness. "I wonder what their story is."

"Maybe they met in college and then went to law school together," Chloe says. She stirs her froyo before taking a spoonful.

"Ms. Talbot did mention once that she briefly practiced law but then decided that teaching was her real passion."

"Wow, that must have been hard," Chloe says. "But good for us that she made that choice."

I agree. Ms. Talbot is an incredibly positive presence in our lives, always pushing us to fight for what we believe is impor-tant. And she's sort of the reason Chloe and I met, so there's that. I'm still not sure what this thing is between me and Chloe or where it's going, but I do know that she's someone I want by my side.

CHAPTER TWELVE

I'm thinking about Chloe the next day after school as I walk across the school parking lot toward my car. Things with her parents are stressful right now, and she's having a tough time. I want to do something to cheer her up. I'm trying to come up with something fun to do, when I see Tyler and two of his friends by a car a couple of rows over. My first instinct is to keep my head down and keep walking. I'm almost at my car, when I hear a voice that doesn't belong to any of the guys. I look over and realize there's a girl with them. It's Maria, a student who just recently emigrated from Colombia. She's a senior like us and quite shy from what I've seen. She's still not quite fluent in English, so she's pretty quiet in class. What're these guys doing with her? I hesitate for a second, but then my gut tells me I need to go over there. My stomach churns as I walk toward them, but I take a deep breath and straighten my spine.

"Are you okay, Maria?" I say as soon as I'm within earshot. Maria nods silently, but I'm not convinced. Tyler laughs derisively, then looks at his friends with his patented smirk.

"Look who's here," he says, projecting his voice like he's an announcer or something. "If it isn't Zara Hossain, defender of the downtrodden."

Luke and Michael laugh like idiots; clearly they enjoy whatever show Tyler puts on for them.

"Some pretty big words you're using there, Tyler," I say with all the sarcasm I can inject into my voice. "Did you download a word-a-day app or something? And by big words, I'm referring of course to *if* and *it*, which are long for you."

Tyler's face registers surprise at my remark, but he regains his composure quickly.

"Why don't you just get out of here, Zara?" he says, his eyes narrowed. He's leaning against his car, chewing gum, and I realize that Luke and Michael are doing the same, like they all share a brain or something.

"Yeah, mind your own business," Michael says.

I ignore them and turn to Maria.

"Let's go, Maria," I say to her. "I'll walk with you."

"Not before I get what I was promised," Tyler drawls.

A couple of things happen in unison. Maria clutches her books closer to her chest, and Tyler moves toward her. I don't even realize that I'm moving, but I step in front of Tyler and shove him as hard as I can. He falls against his car door.

"Stay away from her or I swear I'll call 911," I say, my eyes boring into his, daring him to push back. I can hear my heart pumping loudly and I feel like I've lost all peripheral vision, but all I know is that I have to get Maria away from here. I turn around, take her hand, and pull her away as fast as I can. I can hear his friends giving him a hard time, taunting him, but I can't look back. If I do, I don't think I'll be able to walk away. It takes every ounce of courage to keep walking, wondering if they're following us.

It's only when we're in my car and have pulled out of the parking lot that I feel safe. I ask Maria if she's okay, and she tells me she is even though it's clear she isn't.

"We could turn around and go straight to the office," I say gently.

She shakes her head. "No," she says. "I want to go home. Please just take me home."

I hold it together long enough to drop her off and make it back to my place. Thankfully no one else is home, and I run to my bathroom to throw up. Afterward I sit on the cool tile floor until my legs have stopped shaking. Even though this is hardly the first time I've had an ugly interaction with Tyler, it's never actually gotten physical like this. And today someone else was involved. And I may have just made things a lot worse for her.

Back in my room, I lie down on my bed, the hum of the air conditioner soothing my nerves. I look around at all the stuff on my walls. There's a poster of Fawad Khan right next to a framed picture of Ruth Bader Ginsburg. On the other side of the room is the shrine Ammi has built to me. She says it's to inspire me when I open my eyes every morning. All the medals and trophies I won through elementary and middle school for spelling bees and science fairs are on display, but there are also a lot of pictures of me with Nick from when we got our tae kwon do belts. We haven't gone back to practice together in a long time, and I kind of miss it. I felt that laser-sharp focus today when I confronted Tyler that I used to feel when Nick and I would spar. I'm not even sure what would have happened if I hadn't been there, but I know it could have been bad. I wish I could talk to Nick right now, but then again, I know he won't react well to this. I decide I'm going to talk to Ms. Talbot and see what she says I should do. No one should feel scared to go to school because of bullies like Tyler.

• • •

I try to focus on the essay I have due in English the next day. But I'm finding it really hard to concentrate. The image of Tyler and his friends surrounding Maria like she was some sort of prey keeps flashing through my mind. The way his mouth turns down at the corners when I walk past, like he's disgusted by me. I try to think back and remember when things got so bad with him. He's never really been on my radar. We went to the same elementary school, and I can honestly say I don't really remember any interaction with him.

Zorro comes bounding into my room with his favorite stuffed dinosaur. He jumps up on my bed and walks right over my notebook, steering clear of my laptop. I ruffle his ears as he looks up at me, his bright eyes shiny with pure love. My heart melts, as it has every day since Abbu rescued him from a shelter five years ago. I stick my face in his soft fur and take a deep breath. I instantly feel better.

My phone vibrates, and I grab it off my desk. It's Chloe, saying she wants to meet up, but I tell her I have to finish my essay. We make plans for Friday evening, and that's when I'll share everything that happened with Tyler. I'm glad I can confide in her. I hate telling Nick or my parents anything about Tyler because they get so worked up about it. But Chloe just listens, which is what I really need today.

I feel better when I hang up with her, but not all the way better. I can't shake the feeling that Tyler isn't going to take this lying down.

CHAPTER THIRTEEN

It's almost six when I hear the garage door opening. I'm starving, and thankfully I'm done with my essay.

"Zara, beta, can you come down, please?"

I nudge Zorro, who jumps off the bed and races down the stairs ahead of me.

"There you are, beta. Can you help me with dinner?" Ammi asks as I settle onto one of the stools by the island. "Isabella and John are coming over."

I'm surprised. Aunty Isabella and Uncle John are Nick's parents.

"How come no one tells me anything anymore?" I say. And then I feel foolish because I have to ask, "Is Nick coming too?"

"I'm not sure. But his grandmother might join us."

I smile. I love Nick's grandmother. She gives the best hugs and is an excellent singer. Karaoke nights at Nick's are the best.

"What are you making?" I ask.

"I picked up some mutton to make nihari," Ammi says. "I thought you could make the pulao with some peas and carrots?"

"Sure, I can do that." I jump off the stool to get the rice started.

I notice a pile of mail on the side table. "What's this?" I ask, pulling a shiny envelope from the stack.

"I haven't looked at any of that yet," Ammi says. "Go ahead and open it."

I run my fingernail under the flap and gasp.

"What is it?" Ammi stops chopping cilantro to look at me.

I look at her with a big smile. "Ayesha's getting married," I say excitedly. Ayesha is my cousin in Vancouver. Her father, Murshed Uncle, is Abbu's older brother. I love it when they visit because Ayesha is only a few years older than I am and I've always looked up to her.

Abbu walks in just as Ammi's looking at the wedding invitation.

"Who's that from?" he asks.

"From Murshed Bhai and Seema Bhabi," she says. "Ayesha's getting married."

Abbu's face breaks into a huge grin as she passes him the card.

I spy the slim, intricately decorated box filled with assorted mithai that traditionally accompanies a wedding invitation. I open it eagerly, but Ammi deftly takes it from me before I get the chance to snag a piece of halwa.

"We'll serve those with dessert," she says. "Now can you please go and make the pulao like I asked?"

I grumble to myself as I get the pulao started because now I really want mithai but Ammi's watching me like a hawk.

Nick and his family come over just as I finish garnishing the pulao with raisins and slivered almonds. Nick is holding a glass-covered dish of sopapillas with cajeta, my favorite dessert.

"Abuela made this for you," he says, making a face. "I was not allowed to sample it, and I hate you."

"Finally we're on the same page," I say, turning to hug his grandmother. "Thank you, Abuela. You're the best."

"Kiss-ass," Nick mutters behind me. I give him the finger as his grandmother wraps her slender arms around me and kisses my cheeks. She's the closest thing I have to a grandparent here, since my own live so far away in Pakistan.

Nick's mom is a graceful, petite woman with a sharp mind and eyes that you can't hide from. Nick's eyes are like that, and he has her mouth too. But he gets his height and build from his father, who was also a football player at our school when he went there as a teenager.

Nick corners me in the pantry when I go in to grab some Maggi sauce. His expression has gone from joking to serious.

"I heard what happened with Maria," he says in a low whisper. "Are you okay?"

I'm startled. "Who told you?" I ask. I spent so much energy deciding not to tell him, it hadn't even occurred to me that he'd find out anyway.

"Are you kidding? Dude, the whole team's ragging on Tyler!"

Great. Just what I need.

"Okay, but don't say anything to my parents," I say, pinning him with a stern look.

The pantry door swings open, and Ammi's standing there, hand on hip. "Say anything about what?" she asks.

This day just keeps getting better.

"Nothing, Ammi," I mutter. "It's nothing."

"Obviously it's something," Ammi says, unconvinced. "Why else are you two doing khusurphusur in the pantry? Come on, out with it." She calls Abbu over.

There's really no point in trying. It's easier just to tell them.

"I had a run-in with Tyler again today," I say as quietly as possible. Then I brace myself.

"A run-in? What kind of run-in?" Ammi says, her voice a little high, the way it gets when she knows nothing good is coming.

"I was going to tell you," I reply weakly. I recount the incident with Maria to them.

Abbu looks both sad and angry. "And did you tell the principal?"

"Maria didn't want to make a big deal about it."

"Ye ladke ko to school se nikaal dena chahiye." Ammi has reverted to Urdu, which is never a good sign. She only does this when she's very worked up—and I mean, she's not wrong. Tyler should be kicked out of school.

"Nilufer, it's okay. Zara will report it tomorrow," Abbu says calmingly. "Hai na, beta?" he asks me.

"Yes, of course," I say. I can check with Maria to see if she wants to go with me. Since everyone in our school will probably have heard what happened tomorrow morning, she might be okay speaking up. And if she isn't, then I will find a way to speak up without dragging her into it.

"Good," Ammi says. "Hopefully they will finally take some action."

CHAPTER FOURTEEN

I get a bad feeling as soon as I'm walking down the hallway toward my locker the next morning. Nick is standing right in front of the locker, arms spread out as several students stare at him. At first, I assume Nick's just being Nick and that he's up to something he thinks is hilarious. But as I get closer, I know from the look on his face that something's very wrong.

"Nick, what are you doing?" I ask. "Let me get my stuff—I'm going to be late for history."

Nick shifts uncomfortably but doesn't move away. I put my hands on his arms and try to push him aside, but he's sturdy as a rock.

"Zara, why don't you go ahead," he says. "I'll grab your stuff for you."

Of course, we know each other's locker combo, mostly because Nick always forgets stuff and I have to get it for him when he's not at school.

"What? Why?" A vein in my forehead is throbbing furiously. "Just move."

This time when I try harder to shove him aside, he grabs my arms.

"Can you just go to class, please?" he pleads. "Trust me, you don't want to see this. Priya's gone to get the janitor. He'll have it cleaned off before class is over."

"Get what cleaned off?" I become very still, my body anticipating the worst before my brain can even register what's happening.

Nick knows this look in my eyes and moves aside. My breath catches in my throat as I see what he's been shielding me from.

Painted all over my locker door in white spray paint are the words DIRTY PAKI BITCH.

I can't breathe. I can feel all sensation draining from my fingertips. Every sound becomes muffled and my vision narrows until the only things I can see are those ugly words.

Somewhere outside this bubble I hear Nick say my name. Then Priya's face comes into my line of vision and I'm moving. I feel my legs bending and my backside being lowered into a seating position. I feel a searing pain behind my eyes, and I close them until it subsides.

When I open them again, it's as if the bubble has burst, and everything looks and sounds normal again. Except it isn't, because everyone is staring at me and those words are still screaming at me, telling me I shouldn't exist.

CHAPTER FIFTEEN

When I've recovered enough, I march down the hall to the principal's office, with Nick and Priya right behind me. I can see Principal Trevino through the glass window in the inner office and walk right through, completely ignoring his assistant, who opens her mouth to stop us, but it's too late because we're already standing in front of Mr. Trevino. I thrust my phone in his face, my chest heaving with anger and from walking so fast.

"Ms. Hossain, what is the meaning of this? You cannot just barge into my office," he says, even as he's putting on his reading glasses. His face pales as the words on my screen register.

"Is this some kind of joke?" he says. "What is this?"

"It's my locker. It was like this when I came in just a few minutes ago."

"Did you see who did this?" Mr. Trevino looks at me over his glasses.

"No, but I'm pretty sure it was Tyler."

"This is a very serious offense. *Pretty sure* isn't good enough."

"Are you kidding me?" Nick spits out.

Calmer, Priya says, "Mr. Trevino, everyone knows it was Tyler."

"Why's that?" he asks.

"Tell him what happened yesterday," Nick says to me. "You have to."

I tell Mr. Trevino about the incident with Maria without mentioning her by name; Mr. Trevino surprises me by understanding why I have to keep that secret.

"Tyler was telling the whole team about it ten minutes after it happened," Nick says. "I heard it come right out of his mouth."

"I'll look at the camera footage, and we'll get to the bottom of this," Mr. Trevino says. "I'd also like to talk to the other student involved, if she is willing. Please let her know that her privacy will be respected. This kind of behavior will not be tolerated."

I nod wordlessly. What else is there to say?

"Zara, are you okay?" Mr. Trevino asks, his tone a lot softer now. "Do you want to go see Mrs. Martinez?"

I shake my head. "I'll be fine. My friends are taking care of me." Mrs. Martinez, our school counselor, is nice and everything, but I don't think I want to talk to her right now. What I want is to kick Tyler in the nuts and watch him writhe in agony.

"We've got this," Priya assures the principal.

We leave and head back to the locker area and see that the janitor has already removed most of the slur. He throws me a worried glance as he scrubs furiously.

"Thank you, Mr. H," I say, feeling awful about all the extra work he has to do now.

Mr. H smiles kindly at me. "I hope they find out who did this. This is not right." He shakes his head as he continues to wash the letters off.

Priya and I go off to class, while Nick stays and helps Mr. H.

Luckily, he has a free block and isn't missing any of his classes. Apparently, the office has already notified my teacher that Priya and I would be late, so I don't have to explain. But I might as well have skipped because I can't concentrate on a single word.

When it's finally time for lunch, Nick, Priya, and I meet up outside and walk to our spot together. I pray that we don't run into Tyler or any of his friends.

"I swear if this doesn't get him suspended, I'm going to do something about it myself." Nick is fuming, but I don't need his anger right now. What I need is proof that it was Tyler.

"I asked around during class," Priya says. "I was hoping somebody might have seen him near your locker. But of course, no such luck." She gives my shoulder a squeeze. I look at Nick. He doesn't say anything but just leans wordlessly against the trunk of the tree we're sitting under.

"Do you think they'll find anything on the security cameras?" I ask.

Nick shrugs, looking down at his shoes. "I don't know," he mumbles. "I hope they do, but I'm going to talk to some of the guys on the team and see if they know anything. That paint looks like what we use to line the field. But the utility closet is always locked, so it would have to be someone with access."

In the middle of sixth period, there's an interruption over the PA system. It's the principal, informing us of the incident with my locker and denouncing any such acts of racism and vandalism with a stern reminder that they are grounds for expulsion. He asks for anyone who might shed light on the identity of this vandal to come forward.

The hallways are still abuzz with gossip and speculation as I go to my last class of the day. Many of the students throw me sympathetic glances and tell me that they hope whoever did this gets caught. Tyler and his friends are nowhere in sight. Other than history class, where Tyler was uncharacteristically quiet, I haven't seen him all day.

Just before the end of class, I'm called to the principal's office. Mr. Trevino is waiting for me.

"Ms. Hossain, someone has come forward to identify the vandal," he says. "He is no longer on the premises."

"Really? That's great," I say. "So, was it Tyler?"

Mr. Trevino nods. "Yes, you were right. The camera footage from last night wasn't entirely conclusive, but the witness who came forward was."

"So what's going to happen to Tyler?"

"He will be suspended for now. And the school board will meet to decide if any further action will be taken against him."

"Okay."

So that's it. It's done. But the knot in my stomach reminds me that it's far from over.

• • •

Later that night, I'm lying in bed staring up at the ceiling. I'm exhausted but can't seem to unwind enough to go to sleep. Luckily Ammi and Abbu are out at a retirement party and will be back pretty late. I can't really hide anything from them, and there would have been way too many questions about why I'm so stressed. When I finally do fall asleep, I'm plagued with bad dreams. Tyler standing menacingly over me as he shouts nasty insults. Then suddenly his words turn into actual stones, and I'm screaming in agony as he hurls them at my body. I'm jolted out of my dream to find the sheets damp with sweat. I glance at the clock. It's 5:30 a.m., and I figure I might as well get up because more sleep is the last thing I want right now.

I brush my teeth and go down to the kitchen. A good cup of coffee is what I need. I find Abbu already there. I can tell he's made coffee because the delicious smell of hazelnut has permeated through the whole kitchen.

"Good morning, Abbu," I say, wrapping my arms around him. He squeezes me tight and kisses me on the forehead. Already I feel a hundred times better.

"How come you're up so early, beta?" His forehead is wrinkled with concern, and I want to smooth them away with my fingertips. He worries about me so much that it scares me sometimes.

"Just couldn't sleep," I say, pouring myself a mug of coffee. "Tyler got suspended."

He looks up in surprise. "That's . . . Wow. So, you did tell them about what happened with that other girl?"

"Yes, but there's more. Something happened yesterday."

I tell him about the locker incident.

"My God, Zara! You should have told us right away. This is too much."

"I handled it, Abbu," I say.

"Beta, no one should have to put up with this sort of thing. But I'm glad at least the school did something about it."

"I know. Me too."

He sets his mug down on the island. "You don't look too thrilled about it."

"I'm just worried. He's on the football team, you know."

"So?" Abbu has never grasped the concept of automatic deity status that athletes enjoy in this country. Not that it's so different with cricket players in Pakistan, but still.

"The thing is, Tyler's just one guy. He happened to be the one stupid enough to get caught. But he's got friends, you know. And

I'm pretty sure they all feel exactly the same way. What if they come after me next?"

"Zara, if you don't feel safe at school, please tell me. I can pull you out. There are other schools."

"Abbu, I don't want to change schools now. My college applications are due in a few months. Plus, I don't see why I have to leave my friends and teachers just because Tyler and his friends are racist morons."

"But isn't your safety and peace of mind more important?"

"It is, Abbu," I say placatingly because I know he'll worry about me all day now. "But I'll be fine. I'm just spinning." I slide off the stool and put my arms around him. He holds on to me for a few extra seconds before letting go.

"Maybe don't tell Ammi any of this?" he says before opening the fridge and studying its contents.

I agree. At least one of us can be spared the nightmares.

CHAPTER SIXTEEN

School is hell that day.

Nick and Priya are waiting for me at the front entrance when I get there, but they can't be with me every second of the day. I dodge dirty looks everywhere I go. I'm public enemy number one with some people because I dared to speak up against a racist, hate-mongering football player and got him suspended. Now our school's three-year winning streak will be ruined because its star football player actually has to face some consequences. I'm almost positive that even Mr. Gibbons, our AP Calc teacher, hates me. He usually loves it when I ask questions in class but not today.

Thankfully, Nick and Priya stick close to me as much as they can.

"Jada saw Alyssa walk into the principal's office yesterday," Priya says in a low voice when we're by our lockers between classes.

"Wait . . . didn't she go out with Tyler last year?" I look around to make sure no one's eavesdropping. People have been gawking at me all day, and I don't want any more trouble.

"Yes, but I heard they had a pretty nasty breakup," Priya replies.

"Do you think it was her?" I ask. "Mr. Trevino didn't go into any details."

"I mean, yeah. Unless it was a pure coincidence."

Nick walks up just as the bell rings.

"Have you heard anything?" I say.

"About Tyler?" he says. "Hell yeah, that's all anyone's been talking about. I've never seen Coach so pissed."

"Did they say anything about who ratted Tyler out?" Priya asks.

"Yeah, something about the hoodie he was wearing in the camera footage," Nick says. "Apparently one of his ex-girlfriends bought it for him at a concert."

Priya's eyes widen. "Oh my God, I knew it," she says triumphantly. She lowers her voice. "It *was* Alyssa. Good for her."

"And for me," I say wryly. "I mean, I hate the way everyone's looking at me, but it was worth it."

But by fourth period, I've had enough. I hurry to the washroom before the tears start falling in front of the whole class. I hide in one of the stalls and let it all out until I realize I'm going to be late. I step out and splash cold water on my face. Alyssa walks in just as I'm drying my hands and I freeze. We have history because she used to be really mean to Nick in fourth grade. I brace myself for something mean to come out of her mouth.

"Hey," she says. "How're you holding up?"

She looks into the mirror and dabs pink gloss on her lips while I try to form words. What do you say to someone you've never liked when they're being nice? Everything I think of sounds fake in my head.

"I'm okay," I finally say. "Thanks for asking."

She shrugs. "Tyler's a jerk. It's about time he got what he deserves."

I turn to face her. "So you *were* the one who—"

She interrupts me. "Listen," she says, "don't let it all get to you." Then she turns on her heel and leaves.

• • •

Between sixth and seventh period, I pass Maria in the hall.

She's in the middle of a conversation with two other girls, and I'm happy because they definitely look like they have her back. She sees me, and for a second, I think she's going to stop to talk to me. But instead, she meets my eye and nods.

I nod back and understand: She has her own choices to make.

And, either way, we're both grateful Tyler isn't around right now.

• • •

Later that night, I'm standing in front of the refrigerator, when Abbu wanders into the kitchen.

"Rough day at school, was it?" He smiles and ruffles my hair on his way to the pantry. He rummages in there and emerges with a pack of bhelpuri mix.

My eyes light up, and I grab a half-cut red onion, a jalapeño, a tomato, and a bunch of cilantro from the refrigerator. Abbu wordlessly hands me a large bowl, and I pour in the bhelpuri mix and cut open the little sauce packets that come with it. When Abbu's done chopping the tomato, onion, and cilantro, he adds it all to the bowl. I grab a lemon, cut off a wedge, and squeeze the juice into the bowl. Abbu covers the bowl with a plastic lid and shakes it hard. In the meantime, I take out two small bowls and spoons, and then we're munching on my favorite snack of all time. The crispy chickpea noodles and puffed rice combined with the tang of tamarind sauce and the bite of jalapeño are a perfect complement to the freshness of the tomato and cilantro. We eat together in silence as we often do when we're troubled. I know Abbu is a lot more concerned than he's letting on.

"Beta, are you okay?" he asks after we've finished almost half the bowl. "Do you feel safe to go back?"

"I don't think he's stupid enough to try anything now that he's been caught once."

"Are you sure about that?" Abbu says. "Because I can call the principal and talk to him."

"No, no, there's no need for that, Abbu," I say hastily. "Tyler knows if he does anything else, he'll get kicked off the football team for good, if not expelled."

I know Tyler's stupid but not so much that he'll risk his chance of getting a football scholarship. He must know that's his only chance of getting into any college.

"Okay," Abbu says. "But promise me that you'll let me know if you feel even the slightest bit uncomfortable."

I nod as he grabs both our bowls and gets off the stool. He bends to kiss the top of my head.

"I love you. Please be careful, beta." He puts the bowls in the sink and starts to walk away.

"I love you too, Abbu," I call out to him softly as he disappears up the stairs.

• • •

A loud bang wakes me up. I bolt upright, and for a second, I'm disoriented. I hear Zorro barking somewhere and grab my phone off the nightstand. It's two in the morning. I trudge downstairs, wondering if the noise was just in my dream. But then I hear footsteps outside our front door and the fog clears. I'm wide awake now. Ammi comes down the stairs behind me, her hair ruffled and eyes squinting against the hallway light. The door is slightly ajar, and Zorro is just inside, barking intermittently. I quickly pick him up and put him into the enclosure off the kitchen and go back to the front. I'm about to go outside, but Abbu is in the doorway now, shooing me back. He's holding the cricket bat he always keeps under his bed in case of intruders.

"Abbu, are you okay? What happened?"

"Just stay inside."

Ammi is right beside me, but Abbu motions for her to stay where she is.

"Both of you, please don't come out."

"Iqbal, what is going on?" Ammi pushes past me, and I follow on her heels out the door.

"Nilufer, I told you—"

He stops because Ammi has turned white as a ghost.

"Hai Allah! Who did this?" She has her hands on her head, mouth open, staring at our house.

I follow her eyes and freeze.

On the walls, beneath my bedroom window, the words GO HOME TERRORISTS have been spray-painted in bright red, dripping like blood on the garage door.

CHAPTER SEVENTEEN

Abbu tries to usher us back inside, but we're rooted to the spot.

"Chalo. Let's go inside." Abbu gives us a gentle shove to get us moving. We shuffle in, still in shock. Abbu takes one last look outside before he shuts the front door, locks it, and slides the bolt in.

"Should we call the police?" I ask, but Abbu's already shaking his head before I finish.

"They can't do anything." He releases his hold on the cricket bat, and it falls to the floor with a loud clatter. The sound reverberates through the living room, and I get goose bumps all up and down my arms.

"Did you see who it was?" Ammi is sitting next to him, arms wrapped around herself. They both look as scared as I am.

"It was that boy, Tyler. And some of his friends, I guess."

"What? Are you sure?"

He nods. "I recognize him from our meeting at school. I am absolutely sure it was him. And he could tell too. That's why he ran. Bloody coward."

Chills run through me. When I was worrying about backlash, I never thought Tyler would bring the fight to my home.

"Abbu, are you sure we shouldn't call the cops?"

"Zara, what's the point? There are no cameras, there is no proof."

He's right, I know it. But I want to do something. Abbu puts his head in his hands and stares down at the carpet.

"Abbu, I'll—"

Abbu stands abruptly. "I'm going to go to his house and talk to his father," he announces.

"Now? Iqbal, what are you saying?" Ammi says. "How can you go to someone's house at this time of the night?"

"Nilufer, they came to our home. Who cares what time it is?" Abbu glares at Ammi, and I know this is not good.

"Look, Abbu," I say pleadingly, rubbing his arm. "Why don't we just wait a few more hours? We'll all go. Maybe then his parents will take it more seriously."

"You think I'm going to wait and give that hooligan time to think of an excuse?" His eyes flash with anger. "He knows I recognized him, and I can guarantee that right now he and his father are thinking of some good lie."

"Abbu, please, this is not a good idea. What if he calls the cops on you?"

"Let him do that," Abbu says. "I'm not going to sit quietly while these idiots deface our home. We've done nothing wrong."

I don't know how else to stop Abbu. I watch helplessly as he gets his car keys and walks out the door.

"I've never seen him like this before," Ammi says, shaking her head.

Neither have I. Abbu is usually such a mild-mannered person, but this is far from a normal situation. What if he hadn't heard them when he did? What else were they planning to do? We have a right to feel safe in our own home.

Tyler and his friends have taken that from us tonight.

"Ammi, try not to worry too much," I say. "You know how Abbu is. He'll probably just tell Tyler's dad what happened, and Tyler will get in trouble with his parents."

"Yes, beta, let's hope he comes back soon. If he's not home in half an hour, let's call him and make sure everything's okay."

I go into the kitchen to make some chai. There's no way we'll go back to sleep tonight, and I need to keep myself busy until Abbu's back.

• • •

Forty-five minutes later, I'm on the verge of freaking out but trying to stay cool for Ammi's sake. Abbu's not answering his phone, and I'm very close to calling the cops. I go up to my room to clear my head and decide what I should do. I call Abbu's cell phone and leave several messages, each one more urgent than the last. Fifteen minutes later, I'm in full panic mode. I'm going to call the cops. But then the phone rings, and I breathe a sigh of relief. It has to be Abbu. I run to answer, but the voice at the other end doesn't belong to him.

It's Priya's dad, Dr. Nair.

"Hi, Uncle Rakesh, is everything all right?" I say.

"Zara, beta, where is your mother?" he says. I can hear noises in the background that sound like announcements. He must be calling from the hospital. He and Abbu both work at Spohn South.

"She's here, but . . . actually we're worried about Abbu—"

"That's why I'm calling, beta. You and your mom need to come down here as soon as possible. Your father's been shot."

CHAPTER EIGHTEEN

My stomach drops.

"What?"

"It's your father," Dr. Nair says. "He was brought in a little while ago—"

I can hear Priya's father being paged.

"I'm sorry, I have to go now," he says hastily. "But you and your mom should come immediately."

He hangs up, and I'm unable to move. Many different scenarios play out in my head, none of them good. I snap out of it when I hear Ammi calling me.

"Zara, kaun tha?"

"It was Uncle Rakesh."

"So late?" Ammi calls up from the living room. "Is everything all right at home?"

I run down the stairs and find her sitting on the love seat, a cup of tea keeping her hands warm.

"Ammi, we have to go," I say. I'm still in a daze, so my brain doesn't register Ammi's panicked expression at first.

"Where? To their house? Is it Gita? Or Priya?"

I shake my head. "No, Ammi, we have to go to the hospital. It's Abbu."

She looks at me blankly at first, then comprehension dawns.

"I knew something like this would happen." She jumps up and walks over to the credenza to grab her car keys. "I'm always telling him not to drive when he's upset. Now he's got into an accident, hai na?"

I can't bring myself to tell her the truth and she's already standing at the door, so I quickly put on my shoes and follow her out to the car. As she drives us to Spohn South, it occurs to me that Corpus Christi's one saving grace is that no place is too far. It feels like only seconds have passed and we're there. We park close to the entrance and rush through the sliding doors into the sterile interior of the emergency room. Uncle Rakesh is waiting for us.

"Rakesh Bhai, how is Iqbal? What happened?" Ammi pounces as soon as she sees him. I'm right behind her.

Uncle Rakesh steps forward and explains to us everything he knows—that Abbu was shot in someone's front yard. The police were called, and they in turn sent for the ambulance. Abbu is now in surgery. Uncle Rakesh says he's being taken care of by a doctor whose name I don't recognize, but from the way Uncle Rakesh says his name, I can tell he's a good doctor to have.

As Uncle Rakesh finishes telling us everything he knows, two uniformed police officers come up to us.

"Are you Mrs. Hossain?" the officer asks.

Ammi nods. "Yes, but—"

"I'm Officer Hernandez," the officer says, and then points to her colleague. "And this is Officer Nolte. We need to ask you a few questions, if you don't mind?"

"Yes, of course," Ammi says, "but can I see my husband first?"

I move closer to Ammi, my heart pounding in my throat.

"You can't see him while he's in surgery," Uncle Rakesh says gently. "They said they would come tell me as soon as he's out, and I'll go check myself in a moment."

"We'll try to make this as quick as possible," Officer Nolte says. "Can you tell us everything that happened tonight?"

"We were sleeping, and then there was a very loud noise," Ammi tells them. "My husband went down to check it out and saw some boys running away."

"They vandalized our house," I say, trying to keep my voice calm. I recount the rest of the events to them, right up until Abbu left for Tyler's house.

"And this is a Mr. Alan Benson's house you're referring to?" Officer Hernandez says.

"Yes, the boy my father recognized is Tyler Benson. I've had trouble with him at school."

I tell them about my locker and Tyler's suspension.

"It was payback," I say. "He's angry because he can't play football anymore."

The officers take copious notes while I talk.

"Are we done now?" Ammi says. "I really need to know if my husband's all right."

"Ma'am, we were called to the scene of the shooting," Officer Nolte says.

Ammi's face turns white, and she's squeezing my hand really hard.

Uncle Rakesh moves in to comfort her. "Bhabiji," he says, "Iqbal is in good hands. They assured me that it is all under control. He should be out soon."

"Why was he shot? Who shot him?" Ammi asks the police, her voice weak. Her forehead is dotted with beads of perspiration, and her skin feels clammy to me.

"We are still investigating the incident," Officer Nolte replies. "What you've told us is very helpful."

Officer Hernandez takes out three business cards and gives them to me, Ammi, and Uncle Rakesh. "This is how to reach me. Don't hesitate to call. I promise you, we'll get to the bottom of this."

The officers go away then, leaving us to talk to Uncle Rakesh.

"Rakesh, *what happened*?" Ammi's voice is shaky, and I tighten my grip on her.

"We'll find out," Uncle Rakesh says. "Please try not to worry too much. He's in the best hands, and I will update you as soon as I know more. I've called Gita, and she'll be here any minute. I'll be back soon after I check on Iqbal."

Ammi clasps his hands with both of hers. "Thank you, Rakesh."

Ammi is completely still after he leaves, and I'm at a loss for words. This all feels surreal, like a nightmare, and I want desperately to wake up.

"Ammi," I finally say, "I can't believe they shot Abbu. How could they do that?"

"I don't know, beta," she says. "These people and their guns, nothing is safe anymore." She turns to me, her eyes full of tears. "What will happen, Zara?"

I feel a tightness in my chest, but my eyes are dry. It's not sadness or fear I feel at this moment, but a hot rage burning me from the inside. The image of my father standing in front of Tyler and his dad while they callously shoot him is more than I can bear. I try to push it out of my mind and focus on Ammi instead.

"Uncle Rakesh said Abbu's in the best hands, hai na, Ammi," I say, gently kissing her cheek. "That means he'll be okay."

I want to believe that more than I've ever wanted anything in my life, but I also want to be strong for Ammi. I need to know what happened at Tyler's house. I know Abbu was angry when he left, but he just wanted to talk. What could have pushed things this far?

I pull out my phone and text Nick. I know he's probably asleep, but he'll have to go past my house on his way to school tomorrow, and he'll freak out when he sees what Tyler's done. Hopefully by the time he sees my text in the morning we'll have more information.

"Zara, maybe we should call Shireen," Ammi says. "I think she'll know what to do next."

"Good idea," I say, grabbing her phone out of her purse and handing it to her. I step outside for a moment while she talks to Shireen Khala, who's a lawyer and would definitely be a good person to have by our side.

It's a quiet night with no one around, and I take a deep breath of the cool night air, stretching to try and loosen the knot between my shoulders. It's almost as if this is happening to someone else. My head is spinning, but at the same time, a strange calm has settled over me. It's so bizarre, being here now, waiting while the surgeon removes a bullet from my father's body. How did we get here? If I'd just stayed quiet, none of this would have happened. Now I can't shake the sense of dread that's threatening to engulf me.

A car pulls up to the entrance, and a window is rolled down. I stiffen, but only for a second. It's Gita Aunty.

"Zara, are you okay? Is your mom inside?" she calls out from the driver's seat. She doesn't wait for my reply. "Let me just park, and I'll be there in a second."

She drives away and walks up to me a few minutes later. She's carrying some cloth bags, and I'm pretty sure she's brought half her pantry with her.

"What's all this?" I say, taking the bags from her. They're just as heavy as I expected.

"Just some hot chai and a few things I thought you and Nilufer might need." She cups my chin with her hand. "Zara, my beta, how are you holding up? Your uncle told me what happened."

I repeat the night's events once more and catch her up.

"I can't even imagine how Ammi's holding it together," I say. "I'm so scared."

"Of course, it's a very scary situation," Gita Aunty says. "But Rakesh said they have their best surgeon working on him. And we're all here for you. I didn't wake Priya because of her physics test. But I left a note to call us when she's awake. Let's go in and take these to your mother."

We find Ammi standing by one of the large windows overlooking the parking lot. Her eyes are red-rimmed, but she smiles when she sees Gita Aunty. They embrace, and I pull out a thermos from one of the bags.

"Nilufer, I brought some chai and banana bread," Gita Aunty says. "You should have some. It's going to be a long night."

Ammi sips a cup of chai but can't eat anything. I eat whenever I'm stressed, so I devour the banana bread. Ammi's just about to go ask for an update, when Uncle Rakesh walks through a set of double doors down the hallway.

"I spoke to Iqbal's surgeon," he says. "It turns out that the bullet did some damage, and there was a lot of internal bleeding. It was difficult to repair, but they were able to do it. Now we have to wait and see."

"How long before we can see him?" Ammi asks. She sounds surprisingly calm, but I'm afraid that she will crack at any moment.

"It's hard to say," Uncle Rakesh says. "We'll have to wait and hope for the best."

I've always found this to be such a strange phrase. *Hope for the best.* I mean, who hopes for the worst? Who would hope that someone they love will get shot and then maybe not make it? My parents hoped for the best when they left their homes and families to make a new life in a country surrounded by strangers who would never accept them as one of their own. We hope for the best every day while we wait to get our green cards. We follow the law, give back to our community, and try to ignore the pointed looks and barbed comments that are thrown at us more days than not. But the one time we decide to push back because we simply must, this happens. So right now, at this moment, I want to be able to do more than just hope for the best. But I have no choice because it's all I can do.

Shireen Khala arrives soon after and sits down with us.

"I'm going to talk to the two officers, but I want to get your account of what happened first," she says. "And from now on, you should only talk to me about any of this," she adds.

"Thank you, Shireen," Ammi says. "I'm sorry you had to come here in the middle of the night."

"Baji, please, don't say things like that," Shireen Khala says, clasping both of Ammi's hands in her own. "I'm glad that I can be here for you. You and Iqbal Bhai are my family."

Ammi's tears threaten to spill over, Shireen Khala hands her a pack of tissues, and we go over everything yet again. We give her one of Officer Hernandez's cards, and she leaves to call the officers while Ammi and I wait for an update on Abbu. It's pure torture knowing that he's somewhere in this building, but we can't go to him and let him know we're here.

CHAPTER NINETEEN

Gita Aunty has brought us some toiletries, and she keeps Ammi company while I go to freshen up. My mind is reeling with unwanted thoughts, and I need to keep myself busy. I don't know exactly what Tyler and his dad are telling the police, but I know it can't be good for us. They're sure to spin it in their own favor. It's so easy to paint all the people you don't want to accept with the same brush. That way you can tell yourself you're just protecting your way of life and that they're the ones encroaching upon your space. My whole life I've been surrounded by people who view anyone with brown skin through such a distorted lens that they can't possibly relate. I regret so many missed opportunities to help them see that they're being close-minded, but always in the back of my mind there's been a voice telling me to let it go. But this, what Tyler's done to my father, this is deeply personal. I know there's a storm coming, and I don't care. I just hope I can stand strong in the face of it.

I sense something is wrong as soon as I walk back out to the waiting area. Ammi is sobbing, Gita Aunty is holding her, and

Shireen Khala is in the middle of a heated argument with the two officers.

"Ammi, what happened?" I asked.

"They're going to arrest Abbu," she says.

"What do you mean? Arrest him for *what*?" I turn to look at Shireen Khala. "What is she talking about?"

"Please try to stay calm, Miss Hossain," Officer Nolte says. "Your father has been accused of trespassing and assault by threats."

"Zara, why don't you take your mom over there and have a seat?" Shireen Khala says. "Let me sort this out with the officers."

I reluctantly do what she asks, but I want to scream. The only reason I stay quiet is because Ammi is visibly shaken, and I don't want to upset her further. Shireen Khala comes over a few minutes later.

"It looks like there's nothing we can do about the charges until Iqbal Bhai wakes up and can give them his statement," she says. "I'll call my investigator and have them question the neighbors and see if we can figure out what really happened."

"So what's going to happen to Iqbal in the meantime?" Ammi says.

"He's not even awake yet," I say. "Doesn't he get to tell his side of the story before he's arrested? And what about whoever shot Abbu? Have they told you anything more about that?"

Shireen Khala looks pained. "Mr. Benson is claiming self-defense. He says your father came storming onto their property, yelling threats. He swears your father was holding a weapon— but of course no such weapon has been found. Mr. Benson has been taken into custody, which is a good sign—they're not taking him at his word, at least. But it's conceivable that your father could still face charges for trespassing. What's inconceivable is that they would do anything until he has recovered."

"Self-defense?" I say. "That's ridiculous! He just went there to talk because Tyler came to our house in the middle of the night. And the only 'weapon' he has is a cricket bat that's sitting right now on the floor of our front hallway!" I clench my hands into fists as my eyes fill with hot, angry tears.

"I understand how frustrating this is," Shireen Khala says. "But, right now, that's all I can do. Hopefully someone took a video and we can get a better picture."

Shireen Khala leaves to make some calls, and Ammi and I sit together in the waiting area. Gita Aunty also leaves to get some sleep before work but promises to be back later. I check my phone and see that it's only five a.m. It took less than three hours for a lifetime's worth of my parents' struggles to be undone.

I know Shireen Khala didn't want to alarm us, but I've learned enough about the immigration process over the years to know that an arrest on your record, no matter what the circumstances, is never a good thing. I don't want to dwell on anything negative right now, with Abbu still not out of the woods, but I'm scared of what will happen once he wakes up.

My phone buzzes, pulling me out of my vortex of dark thoughts. It's Nick. He's just seen my text and is freaking out. I update him and ask him to grab Zorro and bring him over to his place. I'm glad his family has our house key for emergencies.

"Zara, can you go and ask them when we can see Abbu?" Ammi says once I'm off the phone. The shadows under her eyes have darkened, and I'm worried about her. It's been a long, rough night.

I go to the charge nurse's desk to inquire, but they still have no update. I ask if they can page Uncle Rakesh because I don't understand why we can't see Abbu even if he's not awake. Uncle Rakesh comes by shortly to take us to the ICU room where Abbu is recovering. His surgeon, Dr. Mehta, is already there.

Abbu's eyes are closed and his face is pale, the veins in his forehead prominent in the harsh hospital light. His skin looks almost translucent, as if he isn't there anymore. I shake off this morbid thought before it burns itself into my brain.

"We had to put him in an induced coma," Dr. Mehta tells us. "But it's only to make sure there's no swelling in his brain."

"When will he wake up?" Ammi asks. I look down to see that she's clutching my hand. I didn't even feel her reaching for it.

"It's hard to know exactly," Dr. Mehta says. "We're hoping it won't take more than a few days. But the good thing is that his body is healing."

Ammi moves closer to Abbu, pulling me along with her.

"Can he hear us?" she says, almost to herself.

"There's a good possibility," Dr. Mehta says. "I'll leave you alone with him for a while, but I'll be back to check in on him."

After they both leave, Ammi lets go of my hand and collapses in the chair beside the bed.

I sit at the foot of the bed, afraid that if I get too close, I'll pull out one of the tubes that are keeping my father alive. I'm terrified. Every coma-related episode of every medical show I've ever watched runs through my head. I've watched them all, because Ammi's obsessed with medical dramas. Almost all my childhood evenings hold some memory of Ammi shushing Abbu as he frequently scoffed at some unrealistic scene from a show. At least that's what I remember from the few times he was home, which he wasn't a lot of the time during his years of residency. Maybe watching those shows was Ammi's way of feeling connected to him, to what he was doing when he wasn't home with us.

I wonder if she's remembering too or if she's just thinking of how she never thought we'd end up here this way.

We sit quietly for what feels like hours, the only noise coming from the machines Abbu is hooked up to. When my phone buzzes in my pocket, I pull it out and realize it's only been thirty minutes. And then I see all the missed calls from Nick, his parents, and Priya. It's seven a.m.

I step outside and reply to everyone. Nick says he and some of the other neighbors have already begun cleaning off the paint on our house. Priya says she really wants to come to the hospital, but she can't miss her test. She promises to let my teachers and Chloe know.

My eyes suddenly fill with tears, and I quickly find a washroom. I go into a stall, and then I can't stop crying. I don't understand why this is happening to us. Once again, I wish more than anything that I'd kept my head down and just let things be. But even now, with my father laid up in the ICU in critical condition, I can't shake the thought that if I didn't stand up for Maria in the parking lot the other day something bad could have happened to her. Abbu wouldn't have wanted me to walk away from a situation like that. But still, I am responsible for this, and I don't know if I can ever forgive myself.

I splash cold water on my face and go back to the room. Room 1630. Somehow, I know this number will always haunt me. I look at Abbu, so small, surrounded by all the large medical equipment. He doesn't deserve this, not after all the good he brings into this world. He has the biggest heart of anyone I know, the most booming laughter that fills everyone around him with joy, and today he was shot down like an animal. All because of the color of his skin. I know with absolute certainty if it had been a white man in the Bensons' driveway tonight, his family wouldn't be standing around him on a hospital bed, hoping and praying that he wakes up.

The rage I've been trying to push down rises up.

I want to punch something, but I comfort my mother instead.

CHAPTER TWENTY

I wake up to the sound of a familiar voice. I open my eyes, and relief floods through me. It's Murshed Uncle. He's flown in from Vancouver to be by his brother's side.

"Murshed Uncle, I'm so glad you're here," I say as he envelops me in a big hug.

"Where else would I be, Zara?" he says, his voice tight with emotion. "Where's your mother?"

"She must be sitting with Abbu," I say. "Come, I'll take you to him."

When we enter the room, Ammi looks up. She takes one look at Murshed Uncle and bursts into tears. We all step outside because Ammi is sobbing loudly and can't seem to stop. I know how she feels. The family resemblance is so strong that except for the extra gray in his hair and the neat beard, it's as if Abbu himself is standing there. After Ammi's composed herself, I take Murshed Uncle down to the cafeteria to get some breakfast. It's pretty empty still, just a few of the night staff coming off their shift and a couple of weary faces that look just like ours, worried and scared for their loved ones.

I tell Murshed Uncle everything that transpired in the last few weeks involving Tyler.

"I can't believe this is the kind of bullshit you have to deal with here," he says, shaking his head. "After all these years, it's ridiculous."

"I'm so scared, Murshed Uncle," I say. "What's going to happen to Abbu?"

He puts down his coffee cup. "Look at me, Zara," he says, in that same tone that Abbu uses whenever I'm feeling down. "We will get through this. I know my brother. He's strong, and he has you and Nilufer to come back to."

"I know, but—"

"No but. Everything will be fine. Bas, that's it. You just focus on that, okay, beta?"

He looks tenderly at me, and I get all teary-eyed.

"It's just . . . I don't know how Ammi will deal with all this. I'm so worried about her."

"We're all here, na?" he says. "She's not alone. You're not alone. I'm here for both of you, and I won't leave until Iqbal is back at home. Okay?" He hands me a paper napkin. "Ye lo now wipe away all those tears. I want to see my bahadur Zara."

My eyes water again from his words and his tender look, but now it's from relief. Years ago, when he and his family were visiting, I'd fallen down and split my knee open. He'd taken me to the emergency room because Abbu was working late. Murshed Uncle stayed by my side the whole time praising me for being so brave. He called me his bahadur Zara because I hadn't cried once through the whole thing.

Back upstairs in Abbu's room, Ammi is still sitting on a chair by his bed. We sit together for a while, reliving old memories from past visits and vacations.

I step out of the room when my phone buzzes. It's Chloe.

Hey, I don't want to intrude. Can I just drop off some food?

Yes, of course. And thank you! Just text when you're here.

I'm downstairs.

Ok be right down.

I run down to meet her at the front entrance. She hands over the two bags of breakfast burritos and gives me a big hug.

"I'm so sorry," she says, holding me tight. "How are you holding up?"

I shrug. "I don't know," I say with a deep sigh. "It's so surreal."

We talk a little more about everything that's going on, with me telling her all the surreal details, like the possibility that my father might be arrested. My eyes are starting to fill up again, and Chloe pulls me back in for another hug.

"I have to get back upstairs now," I say, even though it feels so good just to stand here like this. "Thanks for all the food." I give her a quick kiss on the lips. "And thanks for coming. I'm so glad I texted you."

"Of course, where else would I be?" Chloe says. "Please give your mom a big hug from me."

I wait until she's out of sight before heading back to the ICU waiting area. I make sure Uncle Murshed and Ammi eat a little while I sit with Abbu. Priya and Nick show up after school, and it feels good to sit with them for a bit. Later, Nick's parents come by and update us on Zorro. They say he's been sitting by the front window and waiting for us. But Nick's grandmother has been spoiling him with treats, so I feel a little better.

• • •

Three days later, there's been no significant change, but Dr. Mehta isn't worried and says to give it time. Ammi's face has lost some of the tightness that came from her effort to hold it together, but I'm still surprised when she agrees, albeit reluctantly, to come home with me and sleep in her own bed tonight.

"Nilufer, I will stay right here," Murshed Uncle reassures her. "Teri qasam, hum yahan se nahin hatenge."

Ammi seems satisfied with his promise to not leave Abbu's side, and I drive us home. The ugly words are gone, but it's still clear that something has been washed off. I'm not prepared for how I feel as soon as I walk in through the front door. Even though Abbu's usually not home at this time of day, it's as if the house itself knows that our world has shifted since the last time we were all in here. It's hard to describe, but it's palpable, this sense of loss of something vital in our lives. I remind myself that Abbu is merely in a coma, that he'll be back soon, and our home will once again be filled with his booming laughter. But for now, there's only a deafening silence and it's unbearable.

The police have kept their distance. Over the past couple of days, Shireen Khala has filled us in on the charges Abbu might face. In Texas, trespassing is a Class B misdemeanor, which can mean a fine of up to $2,000 and up to 180 days of prison time. Since Abbu has never been arrested before, Shireen Khala says prison time is highly unlikely. But this is America, so you never know. Different rules for different skin.

It's only a little bit comforting to know that Tyler's father is in much bigger trouble. He's been arraigned on a count of aggravated assault with a deadly weapon, which is a felony that could lead to many years in jail. Of course, I'm sure he'll have the best lawyer money can buy; Shireen Khala is sure that he'll be out on bail the minute it's offered, but that he won't be able to go near any of us if he does get out.

I try not to think about all this and focus instead on Abbu's recovery and trying to give Ammi as much peace as possible. Back at home, Ammi pulls out some marinated chicken from the fridge and throws it in the oven. I busy myself with heating up naan. Neither of us is in the least hungry, but it's something to do until we can go to sleep. We don't bother sitting at the table, perching on the stools at the kitchen island instead. We take a few unenthusiastic bites and then give up the pretense. Ammi makes some chai, but even that tastes like emptiness.

After a while, Ammi disappears into her bedroom. I can't even imagine what she's feeling, and I'm really worried about her. But I want to give her some space, so I don't follow her.

I go to my own room and rummage through the bottom drawer of my nightstand. I pull out a pillowcase I'd started embroidering months ago when Tyler had said something particularly upsetting at school. I'd started feeling anxious all the time, and Ammi had suggested working on something repetitive to distract me. I'd completely forgotten about it, but now I need this to quiet my mind. Nani had taught it to me years ago when she visited, and it makes me feel close to her whenever I work on a piece. I tighten the screws of the frame so the fabric is nice and taut. I'm close to being finished but still need to complete the plumage of one last peacock. The frame is the same one my grandmother used when she first started as a little girl. That first time Nani visited, she showed me how to make tiny clothes, and as a result, my Bratz dolls were the best dressed in the neighborhood.

As I push the needle in and out, filling out the feathers with brightly colored thread, I feel my heartbeat slowing down to a normal pace. My mind calms as the pattern emerges. Teal, black, gold. Teal, black, gold. When I finally put it down, I'm surprised to see that almost an hour has passed. I go to check on Ammi. I don't see her on her bed or in the armchair by the window, so I knock on her bathroom door. She doesn't answer, but there's no mistaking the sobs I can hear.

"Ammi, are you okay?"

It's a silly question. Of course she's not okay. Neither one of us is. But I can't bear the thought of her crying all alone. I knock again, more urgently this time.

I hear her moving toward the door and there's even sadness in her steps as she turns the lock. I enter to find her standing in front of the sink and look at her tearstained face in the mirror. Our eyes meet and mine fill with tears of their own. I put my arms around her, wanting to take away all the pain, but I'm as helpless as she is.

"Zara, beta, please don't start crying now," she says.

"I'll stop if you do, Ammi," I say, smiling tremulously.

Ammi wipes her face with a towel and turns to look at me. She takes my face in her hands and takes a deep breath.

"I don't know how to be without him, Zara," she says, her voice sadder than I've ever heard before. "We've never been away from each other for such a long time. Not since after we moved to this country."

"Ammi, he'll wake up soon," I say, as much to convince myself as her. "Dr. Mehta said the brain swelling is coming down, so it's just a matter of time."

That night, I sleep in her bed, my arms wrapped tight around her. I can't let her sleep all alone in the big bed she's shared with my father for so many years. And honestly, I need it as much as she does, because neither one of us can bear the emptiness that threatens to engulf us.

CHAPTER TWENTY-ONE

We take more shifts the next day; Abbu's condition is improving but slowly. So slowly.

I stop home briefly right after dinner. When I get back to the hospital, I swing by the cafeteria to grab some coffee and find Shireen Khala at one of the corner tables, working on her laptop. Ammi's sitting next to her, holding a piece of embroidery she's been working on and staring off into the distance. Murshed Uncle is on his phone by the window.

"Who's with Abbu?" I ask as soon as I see them.

"Nick came by," Ammi says. "He seemed really upset, so we thought we'd give him some space."

"I'll go and check on him." I hurry to the elevators, wondering why he didn't tell me that he was coming here. I find him sitting next to Abbu's bed, with Ammi's iPad in his hands. He's watching the game. A lump forms in my throat at the sight of my best friend sitting with my father like that, their heads close together, and for a moment it's as if nothing bad has happened, and Abbu and Nick are doing what they love best. A sob must have escaped me because Nick looks up abruptly and sees me standing there with tears rolling down my face. He's by my side in a flash.

"I'm sorry, Zara, I didn't mean to upset you." His red-rimmed eyes are all the explanation I need. "We were supposed to watch the game tonight. So I figured I could come here, and . . . you know."

"I'm not upset, Nick. The doctor said that Abbu can probably hear us. I know he's so happy that you're here." I squeeze his hand. "Thank you," I whisper.

He doesn't try to stop the tears from falling this time.

"Did you talk to my teachers?" I change the subject because otherwise I might never stop crying.

Nick wipes his nose on his shirtsleeve even though there are at least three boxes of tissues in this room. Some things never change.

"I did. And Priya did too. They all said not to worry and that you can catch up when you're back."

"Did you take good notes in chem though?" Abbu wouldn't want me to fall behind while he was here.

"How can you think about school right now, Zara?" Nick's looking at me as if I've grown another head.

"What do you mean? Abbu's going to wake up as soon as the swelling in his brain goes down. And then he's going to feel awful when he hears that I've fallen behind. You know how he is about school."

Nick continues to stare at me without saying a word. Then he shrugs and shakes his head.

"I'll come by after school tomorrow," he says.

I don't say anything as he quietly slips out the door, but I can't help thinking that I must be some kind of monster to worry about my classes at a time like this.

Your education is the most important thing in your life right now. I hear Abbu's voice and I know it's only in my head, but I'm sure that this is what he would say to me if he could speak. *You will always have options with a degree. You never know what life will throw at you, but you must always be prepared, and you must always be able to rely on your knowledge and yourself.*

Abbu's said these words to me so many times over the years that I hear them in my sleep. I know they come from a place of worry and concern, a place many immigrants are painfully familiar with. It's the fear that everything they've worked so hard for could be snatched away in an instant. But your education is something that no one can take away from you.

I watch as Abbu's chest rises and falls, and the rhythm soon has my eyes feeling heavy. I lean back into the chair and let the exhaustion take over.

● ● ●

When Ammi and I pull into the driveway a couple of days later, the first thing I notice is that the wall and garage door have been freshly painted. Inside, we find Nick and his parents waiting for us.

"Did you all do this?" Ammi asks as soon as we walk in.

Aunty Isabella smiles at us.

"All the neighbors helped," she says.

"It's the least we could do," Uncle John says.

Ammi and I have been alternating between home and the hospital, with no time to worry about how the streaks on the wall were a clear reminder of what had been on there. Nick and his parents have been wonderful, taking care of Zorro, bringing us food, and, most important, keeping us company. But this goes above and beyond.

"Murshed is with Iqbal, right?" Aunty Isabella asks. Ammi nods.

"Good, then you can sit and have a proper meal before you go back."

Something smells delicious, and I walk over to the stove to take a peek. There's chili simmering in a pot, and my mouth waters immediately.

"Thank you all," Ammi says, throwing her arms around Aunty Isabella. "I miss eating at my own table."

The doorbell rings, and Nick goes to answer it. It's his grandmother, and she's brought freshly baked jalapeño corn bread. It's perfect with the chili, and afterward we all sit around the table talking about Abbu for a bit.

"Ammi, we're taking Zorro out for a walk," I say when Zorro's cold nose rubbing against my leg reminds me that he hasn't been out for a while. I'm assuming that Nick will want to come with me.

"Okay, but be careful!" Ammi calls out over her shoulder. I know what she's worried about.

Nick and I walk in silence until we've reached the park. There are still a few families around, but mostly it's empty. The sun has almost set, and an orange glow dances off the water as we step into one of the little miradores that line Ocean Drive. Sunset by the water has always calmed me and I come here a lot with Zorro, but today it's not the same.

"Zara," Nick begins hesitantly, "you know I'm here for you, right? Whatever you need."

I nod, the lump in my throat reminding me that I haven't cried yet today. Because crying is kind of pointless right now, isn't it? I don't want to keep any negative thoughts in my mind, but I can't help wondering, *What if Abbu never wakes up?*

That's when the tears come, and Zorro is whining and then I'm sobbing into Nick's T-shirt as he wraps his arms around me in that way that always makes me feel better. Even today when I don't think anything can be good again. I don't stop for a long time, and when I do, all that remains is a seething anger. I know Nick will understand because he feels it too. Especially when it comes to people like Tyler.

"I should have just kept my mouth shut about Tyler." I pull out a tissue from the pocket of my shorts and blow my nose.

"Do you really think you could live with yourself if you had?" Nick asks.

"I don't know." I shake my head. "Nick, I don't know what's happening anymore."

I can't breathe. I open my mouth to pull in air, but it's not enough. My head pounds with every heartbeat. I take several shallow breaths because that's all I can do, and soon I'm hyperventilating.

Nick puts his hands on my shoulders and bends to look me in the eyes.

"Zara, look at me," he says. "We'll fight this together."

Some of the panic dissipates at his words. I relax my shoulders a little.

"Remember what Uncle Iqbal always says: *Don't become a ghost before you're dead.*"

A laugh escapes me at his translation of Abbu's favorite piece of advice for me. Marne se pehle bhoot nahin ban jao. He's always telling me to stop imagining the worst before it happens.

"Do you think he'll wake up soon?" I lean my head against his chest, and he strokes my hair.

"I know he will."

I want to believe him. I need to believe him if I'm going to get myself and Ammi through this.

"We should get back before my mom starts to freak out."

We make our way home, stopping on the way by the bush where Zorro once found a slice of pizza. He insists on checking for it every time we pass by there. It amazes me that he can't remember the command for sit, yet the pizza miracle from months back is permanently etched in his memory.

Nick and his parents stay until it's quite late, and Ammi sends them on their way after assuring them that we are fine.

"Promise to call if you need to talk," Nick says to me at the door.

There's an eerie silence in the house after they've left. I expect Abbu to come walking in through the door any second, asking what smells so good. He sets down his bag and tells us about yet another cute patient he's seen today and shows us a drawing one of the kids made for him. There's always something, but not today. Today there's only an oppressive emptiness, and I'm suffocating in it.

CHAPTER TWENTY-TWO

It's been exactly one week since Abbu was shot, and I'm having trouble keeping it together. Thankfully, Murshed Uncle is still here and helping us cope. We've taken turns going home, to bathe and eat, but I can tell that we're all on the verge of losing it. Ammi's been trying to convince me to go back to school so I don't fall behind too much, but I can't bring myself to pretend that everything is normal, as if nothing's changed while Abbu lies in a hospital bed. Nick and Priya have been amazing, keeping me caught up as much as they can. I keep my schoolbag with me at all times, finding secluded spots around the hospital waiting areas in which to finish my homework. Chloe has come by often to check on us, and the few stolen moments with her help me get through the days. Ms. Talbot's been in touch as well, making sure I'm okay. My other teachers have been pretty great too, giving me plenty of time to make up the work I'm missing.

I watch Ammi as she fusses over the sheet that's draped across Abbu's chest. Freddie Mercury is playing in the background while Ammi works on her embroidery. Queen's always been their jam. In fact, it's one of the things that drew them to each other. I've heard the story a thousand times. Ammi was sitting in the park listening to Queen on her Walkman when Abbu sat on the bench across from her. He'd been watching her for weeks, working up the courage to talk to her. When he finally did, she was sitting with the headphones on and didn't notice him. He waited until she was leaving and then pretended to find a handkerchief on the ground. Every time Abbu tells this story, I make fun of him for being so cheesy. But secretly I love the story of their meet-cute because they're just so sweet together. And I was introduced to Freddie Mercury and his amazing voice as a result. So, it's a win-win for me.

Priya and Nick text me from the parking lot. They want to know if I can grab a quick lunch with them.

"Is it okay if I go out with Nick and Priya?" I ask Ammi. "I won't be long."

"Haan, beta, please go and relax," Ammi says, stroking my hair. "I'm glad at least your friends are able to convince you to leave here for a bit."

We go to Steak 'n Shake, and it's just like all the times we've come here before. Nick orders and inhales a burger and a milkshake, while Priya and I split a large order of Cajun fries and a Nutella milkshake. It feels good to take a break from worrying about Abbu to gossip about people at school. I can tell that Nick and Priya are being careful not to talk about anything Tyler-related and I love them for it.

"It's good to hear you laughing," Nick says suddenly.

"Way to make things weird, Nick," Priya says, scowling at him.

"What? I'm just saying—"

I smile as I shake my head at the two of them, and Nick takes this as an invitation to steal a couple of fries off our plate. I swat his hand away before he can take more, just as my cell phone buzzes.

It's a text from Ammi.

> Abbu's awake. Come quick.

I gasp loudly. "Oh my God, my dad just woke up."

I start to shake uncontrollably, but thankfully Nick and Priya take charge. We make our way back to the hospital, and I run in, taking the stairs two at a time until I'm standing in front of his room.

Dr. Mehta is already in the middle of examining Abbu, so I can't get close to him yet. Ammi's face is lit up, and she doesn't stop smiling. Neither do I because this feels like some sort of a miracle.

"Well, Mrs. Hossain," Dr. Mehta says, "everything looks excellent."

"So, when can we take him home?" Ammi asks.

"In a couple of days, I promise," he replies with a smile. "We still want to keep him under observation. I'd like to do a CT scan and a few more tests just to be sure. So, let me set those up, and I'll let you know shortly."

He leaves, and finally we can be alone with Abbu. He's lost weight, which is hardly surprising given that he's been here for a whole week. Ammi's kept him clean-shaven the entire time, saying that she wants him to feel taken care of. He looks a little overwhelmed but otherwise well. He smiles and holds out his hands. Ammi and I put our arms around him, and we're both crying. It's been the longest week of our lives, and now that we finally have him back, I can hardly believe it. We sit with him and talk for a while, about everything. Abbu is thrilled to see his brother, and we give them some time to catch up.

Not long after, Officers Hernandez and Nolte show up to question him. Shireen Khala is also here. They've been notified by the hospital that Abbu is awake and able to speak. My stomach is all tied up in knots once again as Ammi, Murshed Uncle, and I are asked to step outside.

They leave shortly after, and we rush to Abbu's side.

"What did you tell them?" Ammi asks. "Did they say what's going to happen?"

Abbu takes Ammi's hand in his. "I told them exactly what happened," he says, even in his current state more worried about Ammi than himself. "They said that the investigation was still ongoing, and they can't tell me anything yet."

I pull Shireen Khala aside. "What about the charges against him?" I ask in a low whisper.

She shakes her head. "They found something during their investigation," she replies. "They haven't confirmed yet, but I suspect it's a witness."

"That's amazing," I say. "When will we know for sure?"

"Soon, hopefully," she says. "I know they were questioning the witness this morning. I've also been in touch with the prosecutor who will be putting together the case against Mr. Benton; his team is eager to talk to your father when he's healthy enough. They said the charges against your father are just a smokescreen, part of Benton's defense. I agree. They want to discredit your father because that's the only chance they have of claiming it was self-defense. We just need to put together the evidence proving they're wrong. He's got the power here, Zara, but we have the truth."

I nod. "Let's not mention anything to Ammi about the witness until it's confirmed."

Shireen Khala agrees. "I should know something by tomorrow morning."

• • •

The next morning, I wake up with a renewed sense of hope. It feels like forever since I've felt like this. I go out and get breakfast kolaches from S & J Bakery, Abbu's favorite. He's allowed to eat regular food now, and he's not wasting any time. But I sense that something's wrong as soon as I step off the elevator. I can hear Ammi's voice, and I hurry down the hall to Abbu's room. The officers are there. Shireen Khala is talking to them. Murshed Uncle is trying to calm Ammi down. She's crying.

"What's happening?" I ask Shireen Khala. I'm trying very hard to remain calm in this chaos, but I don't know how long I'll be able to.

"He's being placed under arrest for trespassing," she says. "We knew this was coming, Zara."

"So is Abbu going to jail?" I can't believe I'm even uttering these words.

"Dr. Mehta is not releasing him until he's fully recovered, so no. But he's still technically under arrest."

"So, what do we do now?" I'm fighting an overwhelming urge to laugh and cry at the same time. This whole situation is so absurd.

"My investigator has finally been able to get some information from one of the neighbors, so after I talk to him, hopefully I can clear all this up."

Shireen Khala leaves, and I hope desperately that she'll come back with some good news. Officer Nolte tells us that they will be checking in from time to time, and that the hospital security will be monitoring the room. Officer Hernandez seems genuinely apologetic when she tells us the situation is "complicated" and that it's her sincere hope that when she returns, it will only be to take further testimony for the case against Mr. Benton. I try to take that as a good sign.

When the officers are gone, Ammi and Murshed Uncle leave Abbu's side to come over to me.

"Yeh kya ho gaya?" Ammi says. Her face is wet with tears, and she clings to me.

"Ammi, nothing has happened yet," I try to reassure her. "I know this looks bad, but obviously they won't find anything and then they'll have to release him."

"But, beta, look at him," Ammi says, dissolving in tears again. "Look at your abbu, being treated like a common criminal. How can they do that?"

"Nilufer, sab theek ho jayega," Murshed Uncle says. "It's going to be fine. Iqbal did nothing wrong. Let the police do their job, and the truth will come out."

I sit her down in a chair and kneel in front of her.

"Uncle is right, Ammi. It's going to be all right. We'll get through this. The important thing is that Abbu is out of the coma and the doctor said he's doing well."

Ammi looks at me with a watery smile.

"Shouldn't I be the one telling you this, beta?" She puts her arms around me and holds me tight.

"It doesn't matter who says it," I say. "The important thing is that we have to believe it. We'll get through this. Together."

CHAPTER TWENTY-THREE

I need air, so I take the elevator down. I walk past the nurses' station and wave to Eliza, one of the nurses who's been taking care of Abbu.

"Zara, hold up. I think someone just dropped off flowers for you," she says. She points to a bouquet of tiger lilies in a crystal vase on the counter. Must be from another one of Abbu's patients. His room's been filling up over the past week. I pull out the card and turn it over.

I'm sorry. Never meant for it to go so far.

My blood runs cold.

"When were these delivered?" I ask Eliza.

"Just now," she says. "The guy just left. He might still be in the parking lot."

I run down the hallway through the sliding door into the night. There aren't too many people out here, but I don't see anyone I know. I'm about to turn around and go back in when I see a pickup truck pulling out. It's red with the same kind of design above the wheels as Tyler's. In the fading light of the sun, I can't be sure, but then I see Tyler's head through the window.

He looks at me briefly as he drives away, and I just stand there. Why was he here? And what does the card mean?

I can't decide what to do. Should I share this information with the police? Can it help my father somehow? I'm not sure of anything anymore.

I text Nick.

> Hey, can you come over? Something's happened

Are you okay?

> Yeah but I need to talk

Omw

He's there fifteen minutes later, but he's not alone.

"Oh, hey, Priya, I didn't know you were coming too."

"Nick and I were studying together when you called," she says. "I hope it's cool that I came?"

"Of course," I say, trying not to sound too surprised. Since when do these two study together?

I catch them up on everything, and they're stunned.

"Are you going to tell the cops?" Priya asks.

"At least tell Shireen," Nick adds.

"I think I should."

"Can we go up and see him?" Nick says.

I tell them what happened and that it's probably better if they don't see him right now. There's way too much going on.

Nick's face is dark with anger. Priya looks like she's going to be sick. They've both known my dad forever, so this is hard for them too.

"So while Tyler's father is out on his million-dollar bail, you have to worry about your father going to jail? How is that fair?" Nick asks.

I shake my head. "I have no idea. But I never expected the system to be fair to people like us."

"What do you think Tyler meant?" Priya says. "Do you think he really feels bad, or is this another one of his games?"

"I have no idea," I say. "But I do know I can't trust him or his dad. Who knows what the two of them are plotting?"

"I wouldn't either," Nick says. "Just be careful."

"Yeah, and tell us if he tries to contact you or anything," Priya adds.

"I'm going to take these upstairs and show Shireen Khala," I say. "Thanks for coming, you guys."

I hug them both and head back upstairs.

• • •

Shireen Khala is livid.

"What does this boy think he's doing?" she fumes. "He shouldn't even be coming near you."

She takes the flowers and the card and walks out to find an officer.

"They're going to take it into evidence," she says when she returns.

"It's almost like an admission of guilt, isn't it?" I say.

"Except it's not signed, and he didn't actually say anything specific. But at least we'll have plenty of security footage showing he was the one who dropped them off. The boy tried to hide himself when he defaced your locker, but he didn't this time. That's something. What, I have no idea. But it's something."

"Ugh, I hate this," I say through gritted teeth. "I can't believe he had the nerve to bring this here. I mean, what did he think was going to happen?"

My phone buzzes. It's Chloe asking if she can come visit. I'm agitated and I won't be any help to Ammi in this state, so I agree to meet her outside.

She pulls up a few minutes later, and I slide into the passenger seat. She reaches for my hand.

"How're you holding up? Is your dad going home soon?"

I haven't spoken to her since my dad came out of his coma. I still can't bring myself to tell her about the arrest, but I tell her about Tyler.

"You think he really feels bad about what happened?" Chloe asks.

"Honestly, I don't know what to think," I say. I press my head back against the seat and close my eyes.

"I mean, maybe he didn't think his father would use a gun," she says. "I don't know. Sometimes parents can be so ignorant. They don't how confusing it can be for us."

I look at her in surprise.

"So you're saying that Tyler is just following his father's example? I really don't buy that."

"Sometimes kids try to impress their parents, and if they've been raised in that kind of an environment, who knows what lengths they'll go to?"

I shake my head. "I'm sorry, but I really don't agree with that at all. That just takes all responsibility from the shoulders of someone like Tyler. He's not a child. He sees how the world is, and he chooses to be like that."

"Don't get me wrong, Zara," she says quickly. "I'm not saying what he's been doing isn't horrible, just that maybe he's realizing that blindly following his father's example is wrong."

"I think you're being very generous," I say. "I wasn't there, so I don't know exactly what happened. Maybe he was asleep. Maybe he wasn't. Maybe he had no idea his father was going to shoot my father. Maybe he was standing right beside him. I don't know. But I *do* know that if he had left my family alone, none of this would have happened. Period."

"I didn't mean to upset you, Zara. I'm just saying that things aren't always black and white."

"No, I get that," I say. "But for me, these kinds of things are pretty black and white. You either see people of color as human beings or you don't. And I'm not talking about the everyday small displays of racism. I'm talking about what is happening here today."

I look at her and suddenly realize that she has little to no idea what I'm talking about. I'm pretty sure she doesn't get followed around by staff when she's browsing in stores. And I can bet that no one's ever made a disgusted face when she opened her lunch box. I mean, I get that as a queer Catholic she's dealt with stuff, but she doesn't wear her otherness the way I do. Every day, 24/7, there's no mistaking that I'm from somewhere else. Even if I'd been born here to third-generation South Asian Americans, it's not as if the color of my skin would be diluted enough for me to pass as white. Chloe carries her white privilege with her wherever she goes, whether she's aware of it or not. She can blend in completely whereas I will always be a clear target. And there are so many who're looking to take a shot.

"Zara, I'm sorry, I really didn't mean to upset you," Chloe says. "I just came here to be with you. Should we go get something to eat?"

I shake my head. "I really need to get back up there. Thanks for coming."

As I step out of her car, I can tell I've hurt her feelings, but I just need to be with my family right now.

Walking back inside, I feel spent. It's exhausting trying to explain and defend my reactions to things that happen in my life. And I especially don't want to have to do that with someone I've started to have feelings for. The worst thing is, I sort of get it. Obviously, Chloe's not a bad person. But I doubt if she's even aware of her unconscious biases like so many others who would never, ever consider themselves racists. How can I make her realize how differently I view the world and how it views me? We don't experience things in the same way, and we never will. But it's painful to realize that the way people of color react to hurtful things may appear to be an overreaction to her.

She might see Tyler's flowers as a genuine attempt to convey how sorry he is. But to me it's nothing but a minuscule, totally ineffectual act designed merely to make himself feel better. His flowers and card are not going to undo any of the damage he and his father have done to us. So, thanks, but no thanks.

I will continue to see the world the way I've always seen it. But that doesn't mean I'm not going to fight like hell to make it better.

CHAPTER TWENTY-FOUR

It's two in the morning, and I'm still awake, my dark thoughts morphing into a heaviness I can't shake. Every time I close my eyes, I see Abbu's face and then Tyler's, and I can taste bile. Finally, I give up and sneak quietly downstairs. I don't really feel like talking to anyone, so instead of texting Nick or Priya, I just spend the next hour checking out pictures on Instagram. But all that does is make me feel worse. Why is this happening to us? Why is it that everyone else just gets to go on with their lives while ours is crumbling around us? It's so unfair. This is supposed to be the best year. It's supposed to be a year of new and exciting beginnings. Instead it's turned into my worst nightmare. Although that's not even true. I've never had this nightmare because something this awful isn't supposed to happen. But it is, and I remind myself that it's not just happening to me. My father is accused of something he didn't do, and my mother is upstairs barely hanging on. I know I need to stop whining and get ahold of myself. When all this is over, and I have to believe that it will be over, I don't want to look back at this and wish I'd been stronger. I have to be there for Ammi, the way she's always been there for me. Abbu will be so disappointed if he finds out that I've been sitting here feeling sorry for myself when there's work to be done.

I'm about to go back to bed, when I hear footsteps coming down the stairs. It's Murshed Uncle. Ammi insisted that he come home with us and get a proper night's rest.

"You couldn't sleep either, eh?" he says when he sees me on the couch.

I smile at him. "I feel like I'll never sleep through the night again."

He sits next to me and puts his arm around me. "When you and your parents first moved here, you'd wake up in the middle of the night like this."

"Really? I don't remember." I lean my head back in the crook of his arm, and it feels good. The way it does when Abbu is here.

"Well, you were only three, so I'm not surprised," he says. "I came down here to help you all get settled in."

"It must have been so hard for Ammi and Abbu back then," I say, trying to imagine them so many years ago, coming to a new country with all their hopes and dreams wrapped up with their belongings in a few suitcases. I don't know if I possess that kind of courage.

"I begged your abbu to come and stay with me in Vancouver," Murshed Uncle says. "But he insisted that he wanted to come here."

I don't say anything for a while, content to sit like this in the dark with only a few slivers of moonlight streaming in through the blinds.

"I wonder if things would have been different if he'd listened to you," I say.

Murshed Uncle shrugs. "You can never know," he says. "Who knows if it would have been better or worse?"

A bitter laugh escapes me. "It couldn't have been worse than this."

"At least Iqbal is recovering well, so we should be thankful for that."

I nod slowly. "I am grateful. But at the same time, what's going to happen to us? He's been arrested, and this will go on his permanent record. It's going to look bad for our green cards."

"Don't worry about that," he says. "You do have other options, but I really don't think you'll need them. Your father is not a criminal. Anyone who knows him can see that. And Shireen is doing her best to make sure everyone else knows that as well."

We sit like this for little while longer, each of us lost in our own thoughts. But it's almost morning and we both want to get a little more sleep before we go back to Abbu. As I walk up to my room, I'm grateful that Murshed Uncle is here. He makes us all feel safe, and that's something we really need right now.

CHAPTER TWENTY-FIVE

A couple of days later, we're still waiting to hear whether Abbu will be charged with trespassing or not. Dr. Alter, the president and chief medical officer of the hospital, has come by to say that he knows the police chief and will see what he can do—but we're not really sure what that means.

In the meantime, Abbu is doing a lot better, so I decide it's time for me to go back to school. I'm already quite behind despite all my teachers being incredibly flexible and generous with their time. I'm feeling more positive than I have in the past few weeks. That is, until Priya and I run into Jordyn and Alexandra by our lockers. They're in my chemistry class, but we're not friends or anything.

"Zara, I'm so sorry to hear about your dad," Alexandra says as I'm taking out my lab journal for class.

"Thank you," I say, a little surprised because I didn't really think I'd ever been on her radar.

"It must have been awful finding out that he's involved in stuff like that," Jordyn says. She's smirking, and I realize that I'm an idiot.

"What do you mean? Stuff like what?" I say.

"You know," Jordyn says. "Do you really want us to spell it out? TER-ROR-ISM." She enunciates each syllable, her voice rising as people walk by. They slow down and throw curious glances our way.

My face is burning. I'm so angry, it takes every ounce of self-control not to slap her face. Jordyn and Alexandra are part of the group Tyler hangs with. I can only imagine the kind of bullshit they've been spreading about my family.

"Jordyn, I swear if you don't shut up—"

"What? You'll send dear old daddy after me too?"

"Just shut the hell up, Jordyn," Priya says, tugging at my arm to pull me away.

But the way Alexandra and Jordyn are looking at me makes me realize I gave them exactly the reaction they wanted, and I can't let it go.

"Why don't you run back to Tyler and tell him he won't get away with this?" I say to them coldly. "He and his dad are going to get what they deserve."

Alexandra narrows her eyes at me. "Is that a threat?"

Priya is pulling at me in earnest. "It's not worth it, Zara," she says. "Let's go."

I allow her to guide me away, but my entire body is shaking. I don't think I've ever felt this level of pure rage before. I turn to Priya when we're just outside the lab.

"I can't go in there right now," I say.

Priya puts her hand on my arm, and the coolness is soothing against my heated skin.

"Do you wanna get out of here? We can go and get milkshakes."

I shake my head. "I just need to be alone."

"Are you sure?" She looks so worried that I feel guilty.

"Yes, I'm sure," I say, forcing a smile. "Plus, I don't want you to miss class. Otherwise how're you going to help me later on tonight?"

She smiles hesitantly. "Okay, but if you need me, I'm only a text away."

I walk out to a secluded spot near the parking lot and sit under a tree, soaking in the sunshine and trying to calm myself. But I just can't shake my anger over what Jordyn and Alexandra said. And then I wonder whether I should stop being angry. My anger is warranted, and maybe that's what will get me through this. But how do I stop this rumor from getting out? Does everyone know? And how many of them will stop to assess the veracity of the accusations? I need to talk to Tyler and tell him to stop spreading these vicious rumors. I know his suspension is over and he's on the field with most of the football team right now, because Nick's there too. I walk over and sit on the bleachers. I spot Tyler immediately. I wait until they take a water break and walk over to them. Nick sees me coming and runs over to me.

"What're doing here?" he says. "Aren't you supposed to be in chem lab?"

"I need to talk to Tyler," I say. I can see a group of the guys eyeing me from where they stand. Tyler is there too. I stare at him, and to my surprise, he walks over.

"Can I talk to you for a sec?" he says.

Nick stands up straighter and opens his mouth to answer, but I don't give him a chance to speak.

"Yes, but I have something to say first." My mouth is suddenly dry, and the familiar knot is back in my stomach. But I can't back down.

"Sure, go ahead," he says. Something's off. I can't tell at first, but then I realize his usual smirk is missing.

"You need to stop spreading lies about my father," I say. "Isn't it enough that you almost killed him?"

He turns red, the color rising from his neck like a stain. His friends are paying attention now, and two of them walk over to us. It's his sidekicks, Luke and Michael.

"Everything all right here?" says Michael.

"It's fine. Just get out of here," Tyler says.

"Sure, man. Just making sure she's not giving you any more trouble."

I fight the urge to spit in his face.

Tyler ignores him and turns back to me.

"I didn't say anything to anyone," he tells me.

"I'm sure you didn't," I say derisively. "Jordyn and Alexandra just came up with it all by themselves."

"What happened?" Nick says. "What did they say?"

"They're going around saying my dad's a terrorist." I narrow my eyes at Tyler. "But I'm sure *you* don't have anything to do with that."

"Look, I know you won't believe me," Tyler says. "And I don't blame you, but I really haven't said anything like that."

"Just tell them to watch their mouths," I say, turning on my heel and walking away.

Nick runs after me, but I'm too angry to stop walking. He starts to jog backward as he talks to me.

"Hey, can I come to the hospital after school?"

"Yeah. Sure. Meet me in the parking lot. I'll give you a ride."

The rest of the day is uneventful, but my run-in has left a bitter taste in my mouth. Corpus isn't exactly huge, and people talk. Right now, it's only my school, but soon? Once a rumor like this gets out, it won't be long before my parents hear it. I have a bad feeling that things are just going to get worse.

Priya catches up with me at lunchtime.

"Where did you disappear to?" she says as soon as she sees me walking toward our usual spot by the library. "I was looking for you after chem lab. Ms. Daniels wasn't thrilled that you missed today."

"What did you tell her?" I asked.

"Nothing," Priya says. "She saw you outside and wanted to know why you didn't come in."

"Shit." I'm already so behind, and now Ms. Daniels will think I was cutting class. "I'll go talk to her after school."

"Nick said he was going to the hospital to see Uncle," she says. "Is it okay if I come too?"

"Yeah, sure. When did you talk to Nick?"

"He texted me just now," she says. "Said you yelled at Tyler or something?"

I tell her what happened at the football field.

"I don't care what he tells me," I say.

"I don't blame you," she says. "I wouldn't trust him either after everything that's happened."

"Right? I wish Chloe would understand that."

"What happened with Chloe?" Priya says. "My God, you don't tell me anything anymore."

"Remember the other day, when Tyler brought flowers?"

She nods. "Yeah, that was really creepy."

"Well, Chloe thinks poor Tyler is this innocent baby and it's not his fault that his dad is a racist asshole."

"Are you serious? That's classic white people. When a brown person commits a crime, our entire race is blamed for at least three generations."

"That's exactly what I thought. I mean, Tyler's not a child. I'm pretty sure he knows exactly what he's doing."

Priya shakes her head. "It makes me so mad. We have to keep proving our innocence over and over again."

"For something we never did," I add. "It's ridiculous."

"And now you're supposed to feel sorry for the jerk who put your father in the hospital."

"I swear if Abbu had been the one with a gun, he would be in some detention center somewhere by now. And we'd be deported."

"So, how did you leave things with Chloe?" Priya asks.

I shrug. "I don't really know. I sort of just left."

Suddenly I feel guilty. Maybe I was being too harsh.

"You're feeling bad, aren't you?" Priya says with a knowing smile.

I nod. "A teeny bit, yes."

"You should talk to her."

"Yeah, I'll call her tonight."

We finish our lunch and head back to class. I'm exhausted and can't wait to see Abbu, especially now that Nick and Priya will also be there to keep us company.

CHAPTER TWENTY-SIX

I meet up with Nick and Priya after school, and we pick up pizza on the way to see Abbu. Murshed Uncle and Ammi are there playing cards with him when we arrive. I tell them to go home and get some rest, but Ammi refuses. Luckily, Murshed Uncle is brilliant and says he needs some help shopping for Ayesha's wedding. Ammi can't resist a good shopping spree, so they both go off.

"Abbu, we got your favorite," I say, waving a slice of pizza in front of his face. "Jalapeños, ground meat, and onions."

"Thank you," Abbu says after taking a bite and closing his eyes as he savors it. "I didn't know how much longer I could survive hospital food."

"This is really good pizza, Uncle," Priya says, grabbing a piece.

"Chloe doesn't like onions on her pizza," I say. All three of them stare at me in utter confusion.

"I don't trust people who don't like onions," Nick says, almost to himself. He looks like he's in a food trance.

"So how was school, beta?" Abbu asks. "I'm so happy you went back."

"It was okay," I say. "Lots to catch up on." There's no way I'm going to tell him about the rumors. And for once, thankfully, Nick isn't opening his big mouth and ruining everything. Even he knows that we need to keep this to ourselves.

A couple of hours later, Ammi and Murshed Uncle come back, and we leave. Nick has plans with his grandmother, and Priya and I go to my house to work on our calculus homework. Before she leaves, she makes me promise to clear things up with Chloe, so I text her.

Hey can we talk?

A few minutes later, my phone pings.

Sure

Cole Park in half an hour?

Zorro needs a walk, and he loves the park. I get him ready and head on over. He whines as we walk past Lola and Felix's house. He's been missing them ever since they went camping. We meet up with Chloe and sit close to the water. I let the leash go as long as it can so Zorro can run in and out of the water. He loves to play with the waves, and it's the cutest thing. We sit quietly, watching him as he runs back every now and then with little treasures he finds. He collects them at our feet: a rock, a couple of shells, and some sticks all wrapped up in seaweed.

"Zara, I'm sorry for the other day."

I draw lines in the wet sand with one of Zorro's sticks but don't say anything.

"C'mon, stop being mad at me." She nudges me gently. Then

she picks up a stick of her own and draws a heart in the sand. Then she writes our names in it.

I try hard not to smile. She adds a couple of arrows through the heart.

"Oh my God, you're such a dork." I look at her, and a smile breaks free.

She kisses me on the nose and then my mouth, and her lips taste of the ocean. Then, all of a sudden, we're being pelted with wet sand.

"Zorro. Stop that." I try to sound stern, but I'm already laughing. Zorro takes this as a clear sign of encouragement and goes into Energizer Bunny mode. Soon we're rolling around in the wet sand, giggling uncontrollably. A few passersby give us looks, but we ignore them. It feels good to be carefree again. When it's time to head home, we take a dip in the ocean with all our clothes on. But at least the sand's washed off, and it's so hot that we're dry in no time.

"Zara, listen, I'm sorry for what I said about Tyler."

We're walking slowly, watching the sun set, its fiery orange glow reflecting off the water.

"It's fine, really—"

"No, I don't think it is," she says rather firmly. "I don't want to be one of those people."

"What people?" I say.

"You know . . . the ones who're always making excuses for dumbasses like Tyler."

I squeeze her hand. I realize I'm relieved that I don't have to be the one to point this out to her.

"I'm glad we agree," I say with a smile. "It's really hard, you know. Feeling like I have to justify my anger."

"You won't ever have to with me," she says. "Never again.

I've been thinking about it a lot, and I guess I'll never know just how much crap you have to deal with on a daily basis. But that doesn't mean I don't believe that it's happening to you."

I stop walking and turn to look at her.

"Tha—"

"Also, the next time I say something stupid, please don't shut me out. I know it's not your job to educate me and you can tell me that, but please just don't shut me out."

"I app—"

"You have to promise. I hated it. And I know you're going through so much with your dad and all, so I didn't want to bother you and—"

I pull her close and kiss her. It's the only way I can get her to stop talking. But I also really want to kiss her because she said exactly what I needed to hear and I think I love her. For the next few minutes, I don't think about any of the ugliness in my life, and it feels like a huge weight has been lifted off my shoulders. And even if it's only for a little while, it still feels undeniably good.

Zorro's cold nose on my ankle reminds me that we need to head home.

"How're your parents doing?" she asks, lacing her fingers between mine.

I tell her everything that's happened, and by the time I get home, I feel lighter than I have in a long time.

CHAPTER TWENTY-SEVEN

The next afternoon, Dr. Mehta comes in to discharge Abbu. I'm worried that this will mean he goes directly to jail—but Shireen Khala assures me it's under control. As we'd hoped, the accusations against Abbu are beginning to fall apart. At least two neighbors saw the incident, and neither believes that Abbu was carrying a weapon. The Bensons also have a doorbell camera that may have captured the whole thing—the police have gotten a warrant and are reviewing it now. Abbu's not off the hook, but right now the charges against him are on hold.

It's the weekend, and Ammi goes off to deal with hospital paperwork while I call Nick to give him the great news. He and his parents are there even before Ammi comes back into the room. Nick has the biggest smile on his face as he bends to give my father a hug and there's a lump in my throat as I watch them, but my stomach is just one giant knot of anxiety because I can't shake the feeling that it's not over yet. I take a deep breath and remind myself to savor this moment. The last few weeks have proven that I have to be prepared for anything.

A couple of hours later, Abbu is finally back at home and

resting, while Ammi and I are floating around on a cloud of joy, preparing all his favorite dishes. The tantalizing smell of nihari fills the kitchen as I prepare the raita and pulao. Zorro is running circles around our feet, hoping desperately that a tasty morsel will find its way to the floor. I want everything to be perfect for when Abbu comes down, which should be any minute now since Ammi's gone to check on him. The roti dough is sitting in neat little balls, and I begin to roll them out one by one, throwing them on the tawa until they are puffy and hot. I've already made the borhani, Abbu's favorite buttermilk drink, and it's chilling in the fridge to let the black salt, cumin, and mint settle in.

I hear my parents at the top of the stairs and run up to help Abbu walk down. He's still quite weak, and the doctor has recommended physical therapy for the next month to get his muscles working properly again.

"Why did you two do so much?" Abbu asks as soon as he sits down at the table. "You must be exhausted."

"Iqbal, my jaan, we are so grateful that, Allah ke fazl se, you are back home," Ammi says. "All this is nothing."

"But, Abbu, remember what the doctor said," I say. "You have to be careful not to overdo it. So, you can only have a little bit of everything."

"This feels like cruel and unusual punishment," Abbu says with a smile, pulling me closer for a hug.

Ammi begins to serve the food, and then we're eating and talking like we usually do. Abbu has a lot to catch up on, but soon he starts to fade. He needs to rest, and so I bring him up to bed while Ammi clears the dishes.

"Zara, stay with me for a minute, beta," Abbu says when I've tucked him in. I sit on the edge of the bed.

"Abbu, try to get some rest."

"I will, but first just tell me one thing. How is everything really?"

"I told you, Abbu, things are fine." I don't want to go into too much detail and get him all worked up.

He looks at me closely. "Are you sure? I know you don't want to worry Ammi, but you can tell me."

"Everything is fine, Abbu." I'm surprised at how easily the lie slips out. But my worries about Abbu's health override all my own anxiety.

I leave him just as he's about to doze off and join Ammi downstairs.

"Did he fall asleep yet?" Ammi asks, wringing out the kitchen towel over the sink and shaking it out.

"Yes, just now." I pop a piece of leftover halwa in my mouth. "Ammi," I say when she's sitting next to me, "do you think it's ever going to be normal again?"

Ammi takes a deep breath. "We can only hope, hai na, beta?"

So, that's what it all boils down to. Hope. We can do everything the right way, follow all the rules, work hard, but ultimately it all comes down to hoping that things will work out, hoping that the next ignorant racist who comes at us doesn't do even more damage. Somehow, I cannot allow myself to accept that things will always be like this. They have to change. I have to make sure of it.

CHAPTER TWENTY-EIGHT

With Abbu resting and recovering at home, Murshed Uncle goes back home to his family. I am sorry to see him go, but understand why he must.

As if to make up for his absence, we start getting visitors. Some we don't get to see often, so we're thrilled when they come over. Others, not so much.

Officers Nolte and Hernandez have been over—not to arrest Abbu but to get his side of the story. Shireen Khala is there, recording the whole thing, as they take him through the night. I want to listen in, but Ammi and I are shooed away. Abbu doesn't want us to hear it.

When it's over, the officers look satisfied, and so does Shireen Khala. I take this as a good sign.

Nobody mentions trespassing. I take that as a good sign too.

More visitors come. Chloe's hanging with us, and we're just about to start a movie, when the doorbell rings.

"Zareen Aunty," I say, trying to hide my dismay by quickly rearranging my mouth into a smile. "Assalaam alaikum. Please come in."

"Zara, walaikum assalaam. Masha Allah, you're all grown up," she says, as if she didn't just see me at a wedding earlier this year. "I hope your parents are home."

"Yes, of course, they'll be happy to see you."

I'm lying. My parents don't really like her because she's a pretty big gossip and likes to stir up trouble. I'm sure her being here today is no mere visit. But she came to see Abbu and we always honor our guests.

Ammi and Abbu look up in surprise when I walk into the dining area with Zareen Aunty in tow, but they recover quickly and put on their best host faces. I return to Chloe, leaving Ammi and Abbu to their awkward conversation with our unexpected guest.

A short while later, Chloe leaves, so I go and hang with my parents in the living room. Zareen Aunty is still here, and I can tell that my parents aren't particularly thrilled about this.

"Iqbal Bhai, I'm so glad that you've recovered from your terrible ordeal," Zareen is saying when I walk in. She takes a slow sip of her chai and sits back, clearly in no hurry to leave.

"Actually, Zareen, I'm a little winded. It's been a long day," Abbu says. "I hope you don't mind if I go upstairs to rest for a bit."

Ammi throws him a withering look. Zareen Aunty is blissfully oblivious to his betrayal and smiles at him.

"Of course. Please go and take rest."

After Abbu has abandoned us, we have no choice but to continue to sit with Zareen and listen to her updates on everyone in Corpus Christi's Pakistani community. After a while, she leans a little closer to Ammi.

"I got so angry at Suraiya last week," she says. "She was saying these nasty things about Zara, you know." She darts a sidelong look in my direction.

"What kind of nasty things?" Ammi asks, sitting up straighter.

"No, nothing that anyone will believe," Zareen says hastily. "Of course, our Zara would never do something like that."

"Like what?"

"Well," she says, looking toward the stairs, "I couldn't tell you in front of Iqbal Bhai, but I thought it was important to warn you what people are saying."

"Zareen, will you please just tell me what you're talking about?" Ammi is too irritated now to care about being polite.

"They're saying that Zara is . . ."

"What? Zara is what?"

"A lesbian," Zareen whispers. Then she sits back with a satisfied smile.

I hold my breath. Only my eyes are moving, darting from Ammi to Zareen. Ammi's face has taken on a murderous expression, and I have no idea what to expect. No one says anything.

"Actually," Ammi says, "Zara is bisexual."

I wish I had my phone handy, but sadly I've left it to charge on the kitchen counter. It will be one of my biggest regrets in life because the expression on Zareen Aunty's face is priceless.

"What do you mean?" she finally mumbles.

"Zareen, you should tell that Suraiya to get her facts straight at least. Zara is not a lesbian; she's bisexual. In fact, that girl Chloe who was here when you arrived is Zara's girlfriend. I would think your concern would be with the fact that my husband was *shot*, not that my daughter is in love."

Zareen opens her mouth and then closes it. Her eyes bulge out of her face.

"You mean you are okay with all this?" she asks after gulping in a lot of air.

"Yes, why wouldn't we be?" Ammi says innocently.

"You mean you *and* Iqbal Bhai? He's okay with this too?"

"That's right."

"But how . . . astaghfirullah, Nilufer, this is haram. How can you let your daughter do something like that?"

Ammi's eyes are blazing with anger as she stands and towers over Zareen.

"Zareen, who the hell do you think you're talking to? How dare you talk about haram and my daughter in the same sentence?"

Zareen stands as well, clearly not intimidated by Ammi.

"Nilufer, what she's doing is against our beliefs," she says. "It is a sin. And by allowing her to continue like this, you are also committing a sin."

"*Zareen.*" A thunderous voice comes from the staircase. We all turn our heads to see Abbu coming down. "How dare you come into my home and insult my family like this?"

Abbu walks over and stands by my side. He puts his arm around my shoulders and squeezes.

Even with all the blush, I can tell that Zareen's face has lost some of its color. "Iqbal Bhai, I didn't mean—"

"Didn't mean what? Please take your outdated and narrow-minded beliefs and leave. And tell anyone else who has an opinion about my family that if I hear them saying anything about my daughter, they will have to deal with me."

Ammi walks swiftly to the front door and opens it.

"Just in case it wasn't clear, you are not welcome in our house."

Zareen throws a death glare in my direction before turning on her heel and marching out the door.

I release the breath I'd been holding. My eyes well up, and I pull Ammi and Abbu into a tight hug.

CHAPTER TWENTY-NINE

"She said *what*?" Chloe shakes her head. "What a bitch."

"I wish you could have seen her face when my mom told her off," I say with a huge grin. We're in the park the next day, watching the sun set. "It was priceless."

"What do you think's going to happen?" Chloe says.

"Who knows. She's probably telling everyone that she always knew we're not *real* Muslims."

"Well, if my parents supported me the way yours did, I can bet there'd be a few people who'd say we weren't real Christians," Chloe says.

"I honestly don't understand why people can't just mind their own business." I take a bite of my Mars bar.

"How much chocolate are you going to eat?" She tries to pry the bar out of my hands, but I swat her arm playfully.

"Mind your own beeswax. I'm getting my period."

"Well, do you have any more in there?" she asks, pointing her chin at my bag. "I think I'm getting mine too."

I root around and produce a Twix bar. She takes it, tears open the wrapping, and begins munching on it.

"So," Chloe says, an incredibly goofy grin lighting up her face, "your mom said we're girlfriends?"

"Yeah, but that was only—"

"Well," she says, leaning back, "I wouldn't want your mom to be wrong. You know what I mean?"

I lean over to her and break off a piece of her Twix. "Yeah, I know what you mean."

Chloe smiles. "Now, that wasn't so hard, was it?"

I kiss her, then say, "No, not at all."

• • •

A loud noise wakes me up later that night, and I sit up straight in bed. All my senses are on high alert. This cannot be happening again. Then I hear Abbu's voice. It's loud, but I can't make out what he's saying. I run into my parents' bedroom to find Ammi sitting up and gently stroking Abbu's head. His eyes are closed, so I walk softly to Ammi's side.

"It was just a nightmare," Ammi whispers. "He knocked over the brass bowl."

"Are you okay?" I ask her. The light from her bedside lamp casts dark shadows on her face, and it looks strained.

"I'm fine, beta. Go to sleep. It's okay."

I squeeze her hand and stay for a few minutes until Abbu's sound asleep again and snoring gently. Ammi looks worried but she gets back under the covers, so I tiptoe to my room.

I find it hard to go back to sleep. Every time I close my eyes, I see images of Tyler's dad standing over Abbu and shooting him. And I can't help thinking that if I'm experiencing this, how much worse it must be for Abbu all the time now. I toss and turn for hours until I finally fall into a restless sleep.

• • •

The next morning, both my parents look exhausted. It's the weekend, and I decide that we need to do something fun. I call Nick, and we quickly come up with a plan. We're going to have a game night and then maybe watch some movies. When I tell Ammi and Abbu, they decide to invite Priya and her parents as well as Shireen Aunty. I love a good party, so I'm game. Ammi decides to make goat biryani, so I defrost the meat while she starts chopping onions and green chilies. Abbu tries to help, but we quickly shoo him out of the kitchen. There's a game on, and I set him up on the couch with a blanket and a cup of chai. A little bit later, Nick waltzes in and makes a beeline for the leftover paranthay and eggs from breakfast.

"What're you doing here?" I ask him. "I thought you were coming later."

"Your dad called me to watch the game with him," he says. He takes his plate and walks over to join Abbu.

"Priya's coming too," I call out to him as I separate cilantro leaves from the stalks.

Nick's head pops up. He has a huge smile on his face.

"Really?"

"Yes," I say. "Why? What's the big deal?"

"Nothing." He slides back down on the couch.

"Your father looks very happy," Ammi says, smiling in Abbu's direction. "Good thing Nick came over." She lowers her voice slightly. "He woke up a few more times last night."

"You look like you barely got any sleep either," I say. "Is this too much for today?"

"Nahin, nahin, I'm glad we're doing this. We all need the distraction," she says. "Plus, I wanted to invite everyone over anyway to thank them for helping us out at the hospital."

"Yes, I can't imagine how we would have gone through it without them."

"They are truly our family," Ammi says. "Otherwise, when Abbu and I came here, we had no one, and if it wasn't for all of them . . ." Her voice trails off as she's lost in her memories of another time. Sometimes I marvel at the courage it must take to pack up your life and move thousands of miles away from your home, your family, and everything familiar. It couldn't have been easy to start a new life in a strange place with nothing to call your own. But they've built an amazing life here, full of friends who've become family, and I realize that I should never take it for granted.

The doorbell interrupts my musings, and I quickly turn on the rice cooker before going to answer the door. It's Priya and her parents. Gita Aunty has brought coconut fish, her Kerala specialty dish. My mouth waters in anticipation of the spicy, tangy flavors of tamarind and red chilies. Priya walks in behind her mom bearing a large platter full of appam, the fermented rice pancakes that Abbu loves. Nick jumps up and rushes to the kitchen to help her. He must think her arms are broken or something. What other reason could he have for suddenly being so helpful, when he's spent the last hour with his butt glued to the couch? I make a mental note to ask him about this later.

Shireen Khala arrives minutes later with a tray of tandoori chicken and her delicious kheer. Nick's parents and grandmother are the last to arrive. They've brought chicken mole and warm tortillas, as well as dessert. Ammi's biryani is almost done, and soon we're all sitting at the dining table for a late lunch. The food is delicious, and it almost feels like the horrors of the past few weeks never happened. Almost. After lunch Nick grabs a bucket of vanilla ice cream from the freezer. We eat it with the chocolate chimichangas his grandmother made for us. It is mind-blowingly delicious. Unfortunately, the good times come to an end as our guests take their leave one by one. Only Shireen Khala stays behind, and I can tell it's time to get back to reality.

"Iqbal Bhai, we have to talk," she says after everyone's gone and all the food and dishes have been put away.

Ammi makes coffee for everyone, and we sit in the living room.

"I've spoken to the prosecutor who has been assigned your case," she begins. "Dr. Alter's relationship with the police chief was helpful in delaying any charges. But you are now being officially charged with trespassing."

"So he has to go to jail?" Ammi asks. "But he is still recovering. How will—"

"Actually," Shireen Khala interrupts, "because it's a misdemeanor and not a felony, we were able to prevent that. Even more important, the prosecutor is very sympathetic to the situation. Unfortunately, there may be no way around the trespassing charge—Iqbal Bhai did technically trespass on the Bensons' property. But as I said, the prosecutor is sympathetic. If we put in a guilty plea, there will be no jail time, only a small fine. That is the offer. I suggest we take it."

Abbu is lost in thought. His face isn't as gaunt as when he came back from the hospital, but I can see the worry in his eyes.

"What about Benson?" he asks. "He shot me. Will he serve any time?"

"I believe he will," Shireen Khala says. "But I must caution you . . . with the evidence that's been gathered, I suspect he will make a plea as well. He is very rich and well connected, so the jail time he serves might not be what we want it to be. It will be something but not enough."

"Of course." Ammi's tone has a bitterness I rarely hear. But I feel the same way.

"Okay, then," Abbu says, abruptly getting up. "I think I need to rest now."

He shuffles slowly up the stairs, declining my offer to help him. It seems our window for a little joy has closed once again.

CHAPTER THIRTY

Abbu's hearing before the judge is a week later, and I have a calculus and a chemistry test, so Ammi doesn't want me to come. I think she secretly doesn't want me there in case things don't go our way and Abbu is hauled off to jail. I try to stay positive and focus on my tests, but it's really difficult. I don't know if Ammi will be able to handle this after everything she's been dealing with already. And I can't even think about what will happen to Abbu in there.

I have a free study block after my chem test and I don't want to be around anyone, so I go to sit under my tree by the parking lot. I'm lost in thought wondering what's happening in court right now, when a shadow blocks the sun. I look up to see Tyler Benson standing over me. I get to my feet immediately, blood rushing to my head at a dizzying speed.

"Zara, can I talk to you for a minute?" he says. He looks different, wilted somehow compared to his usual arrogant self. The swagger is missing, but I'm not letting down my defenses.

"What do you want?"

He hesitates, scrunching up his face. He opens his mouth, but nothing comes out.

I say, "Look, I don't—"

"I didn't know my dad was going to do that."

I freeze.

"What?"

"I . . . He's always been . . . Never mind, what I'm trying to say is I'm really so sorry. I had no idea things would get so bad."

I'm not sure how I'm supposed to feel right now. I don't feel anything. Tyler's words ring hollow.

"You don't have to say anything," he says. "I wouldn't believe me either, and I don't blame you for hating me." Then he adds quietly, "I hate myself too." He says it so softly that I'm not even sure if I've heard him right.

I can't bring myself to say anything to him because I have this irresistible urge to scream and claw at his face. How is this supposed to help? And then it dawns on me: He isn't trying to help me. He's just trying to assuage his own guilt for the role he played in almost getting my father killed and destroying our lives. Well, I'm not going to help him or make it easy for him. I don't even care if that makes me a bad person. I'm okay with that because I don't owe him anything.

I walk away, leaving him standing there, alone in his pathetic pool of guilt. I hope he drowns in it.

● ● ●

A few minutes later, I get a call from Ammi.

"It's done," she says. "No jail, just a small fine. We'll see you after school."

When I get home, Abbu and Ammi are waiting with Shireen Khala. I'm expecting a celebration, but the mood is grim. My father, a kind, caring man who has helped thousands of sick children and their families, who has volunteered and raised money for the Corpus Christi community, who never hesitated

151

to help anyone in need, has had to plead guilty in a court. What that means is fully hitting me now.

They fill me in on what happened, about how they were lucky they got the judge that they got, and how it was over in a matter of minutes. The only penalty was a two-hundred-dollar fine, and if Abbu stays out of trouble for the next two years, his record will be cleared.

"It was a good deal," Shireen Khala assures me. "A very good deal."

Then she continues. "Still . . . we have to talk about your green card application. This misdemeanor will be on your record for the next two years, and while it is not a felony charge, which would mean a lot of trouble, the climate being what it is, we can't be sure how a misdemeanor will be taken."

"Will they consider the circumstances?" Ammi asks.

"It depends," Shireen Khala replies. "If we get a lenient immigration judge, it is possible. But we can't count on that."

"So, what do you suggest we do?" Abbu asks.

"There are several options," Shireen Khala says. "But I do want to encourage you to start making alternate plans."

"What does that mean exactly?" I ask. "Are you saying that we might never get our green cards?"

"I'm sorry, but that is a distinct possibility," she says. "Part of the condition of your immigration status is that there cannot be any sort of criminal offense."

"It's a criminal offense to want to protect your family?" Ammi says with a bitter laugh.

I know her outrage is not directed at Shireen Khala, and I know exactly what she's feeling. Panic is rising in me as well. Suddenly it feels like the walls are closing in on me and I can't breathe. I look at Abbu, and he's quiet, just sitting there, an odd expression on his face.

"We should just go home," he says suddenly.

Ammi and I both stare at him.

"What? Where?" I say.

"Home," he says. "Back to Pakistan."

I'm too stunned to speak.

"You know, Iqbal," Ammi says, "I've been thinking about this since you were in the hospital."

"You never said anything," he says softly to her.

"I didn't want you to worry," Ammi says. "But I don't think I can ever feel safe here again."

He pulls her close, and I think they've forgotten that Shireen Khala and I are still here.

"Let's see what happens in the next few weeks," Abbu says. "We don't have to make any decisions now."

"It would be nice to be close to everyone again," Ammi says, her eyes distant. My panic has reached a critical level, but I don't have the right words to express how I feel at this moment, so I say nothing. I don't want to do anything to upset my parents when they're already so worried.

Shireen Khala coughs discreetly. "Why don't I leave you to think about it and we can talk again in a couple of days," she says. "In the meantime, please call me if you need anything."

She leaves and I go up to my room. I have to figure out what I'm going to do. It's as if everything is changing too fast and I can't keep my balance. I can't afford to fall, not now, not when my future is at stake. I know it might not happen at all, but I have to decide if I'm willing to leave my whole life behind and go back to Pakistan with my parents. And if I'm not, what will I lose instead?

CHAPTER THIRTY-ONE

Since Abbu is still recovering at home and Ammi's there to look after him, I decide to get back into school and SJC with full force. With the help of my friends and teachers, I manage to complete all my work and take missed tests before too long. And it's great to get back into SJC stuff and to talk to Ms. Talbot again. It's good to think about something other than my family's precarious immigration status, so instead I focus all my pent-up anger on SJC. There's an event organized by a mosque in Victoria this upcoming weekend. It's an open community event intended to foster better awareness and communication for everyone.

Unfortunately, the event's social media page is already full of vile comments from trolls threatening a variety of things they will do to stop it from being carried out peacefully. Ms. Talbot spends a great deal of time at the meeting making sure we're aware of the risks involved in going. She's mostly concerned about the presence of a particular "patriot" group who has demonstrated extreme anti-Muslim sentiments in the past. But regardless, we're all determined to go. Most of the people here know what my family's been through, so they're eager to take a stand.

We assemble early in the morning at our designated meeting place and get on the bus that Ms. Talbot has arranged for the ninety-minute trip to Victoria. She's even brought breakfast burritos, croissants, and coffee for us. By the time we get there, we're energized and ready, although I'm sad that Chloe had to back out at the last minute. Her parents were worried about her safety and refused to let her come.

People are congregated outside the mosque. I look around trying to spot anyone who looks shady, but it's still pretty early. Ms. Talbot talks to a couple of the security guards who are stationed around the area. They escort us into the fenced parking lot. We are here only to show support if any anti-Islamic groups show up. We've come prepared with signs as always, but unlike the last event we went to, nothing is happening here yet.

I notice some people come toward the fenced area where we're standing. It looks like a group of students like us. It saddens me to think that some people think of activism as a way to stop others from living their lives in peace.

The group that sauntered up to us stops on the other side of the fence.

"So, do you guys support all this?" one of them asks.

"Standing against terrorism and hatred?" I ask. "Sure, don't you?"

She looks confused. "But they're the ones who are the terrorists and they're the ones spreading the hatred."

I stare at her in Muslim.

"You can't possibly think that all Muslims are terrorists." I'm trying hard not to sound condescending, but I don't think it's working.

"Well, they're trying to bring Sharia law into our country, and we're not going to stand for it," one of the guys in the group says.

Nick pulls out a bunch of informative pamphlets we've prepared for just such an occasion and slides them through the gaps in the chain-link fence.

"Here, why don't you guys pass these out and read them?" he says with a friendly smile. It's a good thing they don't know that beneath his smile is a tired disdain for people like this.

They leave the papers on the ground and walk away. I guess you can't make people see reason if they're hell-bent on staying ignorant.

In the end, the patriot group never shows up, and the event takes place without any real protest, other than a handful of people on the other side of the fence shouting weakly about the evils of Sharia law and Muslims invading their homeland. We return to Corpus, heartened by the fact that, after all the trolling, this event was held without too much resistance after all.

"Do you feel like doing something after?" Nick asks me when we're on the bus home. "Priya and I were going to watch a movie and then grab dinner. Or do you have plans with Chloe?"

I had planned to talk to all three of them tonight about how my parents were considering moving back to Pakistan. But right now, I'm more curious about the fact that Nick and Priya have made plans to hang out. By themselves. This is very interesting.

"Since when do you two make plans together?" I ask, trying my best to sound nonchalant.

"What do you mean?" Nick asks. "We're just hanging out like we always do."

Okay, so that's how we're going to play it. That's cool. I'm down with that.

"Sure, what movie are you guys thinking of?"

Nick and Priya exchange a quick look.

"Umm, we were thinking of watching *To All the Boys I've Loved Before*," Priya says. "But we can pick something else if you want," she adds quickly.

"No, no that's fine," I say. "You know I love Noah Centineo."

We're starving, so we go for tacos first. I can't shake the feeling that I'm a third wheel. How long have I been gone?

I tell them about my encounter with Tyler. They're stunned.

"I can't believe he thinks he can just apologize and put the blame on his father," I say.

Priya gives me a look.

"What?" I ask. I know that look. I don't like that look.

"Nothing," she says. "I just think that maybe he does feel bad."

"What does that even mean?" I say wearily. "What does he feel bad about? Being an asshole? Or that his father is an even bigger asshole and they're both just plain evil?"

"Zara, I think what Priya's trying to say is that maybe Tyler's father really is a piece of work. I've heard the guys talking about it on the team. Apparently, his mom left because she couldn't take it anymore."

"So now I'm supposed to feel sorry for him and forgive him because the poor baby didn't know it's wrong to treat people like crap?"

I can't believe the two of them don't get it.

"Zara, it's just . . . you've been so angry lately," Priya says. "And of course you have every reason to be. We're angry too."

"But we feel like it's taking over," Nick says. "We just want to help you move on."

"I mean, look," Priya says, "Uncle is at home and things are starting to get back to normal now, right?"

I feel hysterical laughter bubble up inside. Normal? Nothing about any of this is normal.

"You know what? I think I need to be alone right now. You guys go ahead and enjoy the movie."

"Come on, Zara, don't be like that," Nick says. "You know we're just trying to help. You don't have to get all sulky." Nick knows he can get away with talking to me like this. He knows me a little too well. But this is different.

"I'm not sulking, really," I say. "Listen, both of you. I know you've got my back. But I really need to just focus on school and my parents right now."

They drop me off at home, and I go straight up to my room. I'm exhausted and my mind is swirling with all kinds of stuff. Eventually I fall into a restless sleep, plagued by thoughts of fighting this battle all by myself.

CHAPTER THIRTY-TWO

"Zara, beta, can you come here for a minute?" Abbu calls to me just as I'm getting ready for another sparring session with Mr. Clair.

Tae kwon do is helping me stay sane through all of this, keeping my anxiety at bay. Otherwise, I worry that I'll have some sort of a meltdown right in the middle of a test or something. None of us have talked again about going back to Pakistan. At least not in a conversation I've been part of. I can't be sure if Ammi and Abbu have been discussing it.

We have settled into a new sort of routine. Abbu's almost fully recovered but not to the point that he can go back to work—it's going to be a while before he can be exposed to his patients' sicknesses. Because of this, he's getting restless. This is the longest he has ever been home in fourteen years.

"Coming, Abbu," I call out. I quickly grab my tae kwon do bag and drop it at the top of the stairs before entering my parents' bedroom.

Abbu waves me over. "Where's your mother?" he whispers.

"I think she's in the study," I say. "Why are you whispering?"

"Have you noticed her acting strangely at all?" he asks.

"I mean, no more than usual," I say with a grin.

"I'm serious, Zara," he says. "I'm worried about her. She hasn't been sleeping well at all, but whenever I ask her about it, she changes the subject."

"I'll talk to her," I say. "Don't worry so much, Abbu. After everything that happened, it's going to take some time. And you know how Ammi gets."

My mother has always been overprotective of Abbu and me. It's how she shows her love, by worrying herself sick every time we step out of the house. But I have to admit that I haven't been paying too much attention lately, what with all the catching up at school and trying to keep myself from falling into the dark abyss of depression and anxiety.

I find Ammi in the kitchen.

"Ammi, I'll be back late," I say, grabbing a bottle of water from the refrigerator.

She wipes her hand and tucks a strand of hair behind my ear.

"It's so late, beta," she says. "Where are you going?"

"It's seven thirty, Ammi," I say. "I'm going to the rec center to spar with Mr. Clair. And then I'm going to the library to study."

"Okay, but can you text me when you're leaving the rec center and then again when you're at the library?"

"Sure, Ammi, but why are you so worried? It's not even dark out."

"I know, but I just worry these days," she says. "Just text me, okay? Please."

"I will, I promise."

A couple hours later, I'm in one of the study carrels, working on my college admission essays. I stay until the library closes and then head on home.

I walk in to find Ammi pacing back and forth, phone in her hand, looking frantic.

"Ammi, what happened?" I ask, rushing to her. "Is Abbu okay?"

"Where have you been?" she yells. "You were supposed to text me! And why weren't you answering your phone?"

"Oh my God, Ammi, I'm so sorry." I put my arms around her and squeeze gently. "I threw my phone in my gym bag after sparring, and I forgot to take it out."

"Zara, how can you be so careless?" She leans away from me. "I've been worried sick. And I couldn't say anything to Abbu because I don't want him to get worked up too."

"I'm really sorry, Ammi. I promise I won't forget again." I feel awful. Especially right after Abbu told me that he was concerned about her.

"You don't understand how scared I am every time you're out late," Ammi says, sinking to the couch.

"But what are you scared about? I wasn't alone or anything. The library is full of people."

"And what will they do if someone points a gun at you?" she asks.

I get what she's afraid of. But still. "Ammi, we can't live in fear like that," I say. "Because then we're letting them win."

Ammi sits back, and I realize she's somehow aged a hundred years in the last month. I smooth her hair and kiss her cheek. Then I just sit with her, our breaths harmonizing, and it feels good. It's going to be a long time before we can be at peace again and it's going to take a real effort to make our lives normal again. But for now, I want to just be a source of strength for both my parents, just like they've always been for me.

CHAPTER THIRTY-THREE

My phone pings a couple of days later. It's Chloe. We've both been pretty busy with school, so we haven't really had a chance to hang out much.

Can I come over?

Sure. Is everything ok?

I had a huge fight with my parents. I need to get out of here.

Just bring some of your stuff. You can stay with us.

Are you sure? What about your parents?

Don't worry about them. Just come.

I find my mom in the kitchen listening to old Hindi songs as she chops onions. I'm not sure if it's the onions or the songs that are making her cry.

"Ammi," I say, popping my head in, "is it okay if Chloe stays over tonight?"

Ammi looks up, tears streaming down her face.

"Yes, of course. When is she coming? Before dinner?" Ammi puts down the knife, walks over to the fridge, and begins to rummage for potential dinner ingredients.

"In a little bit. But I want to tell you something before she gets here."

"Haan, beta, bolo, what is it?"

"Chloe had a fight with her parents, and she doesn't want to be there anymore."

Ammi tilts her head sympathetically. "Bechari bachchi, do you know what happened?"

I hesitate. But it's better for Ammi to know what's going on.

"She came out to her parents last year, and they're not taking it well. She says they make her feel like she's sick and has to be cured."

"Poor child. I'm glad you told me, beta."

And that's it. As far as Ammi is concerned, if she needs us, then we will be there for her. I often count my blessings that my parents are the way they are. It doesn't escape me that I'm one of the lucky few. I come from a culture that can be ultra-conservative about certain things and a country where being bisexual could land me in jail or worse. But my parents have never made me feel that I've disappointed or embarrassed them in any way. What they *have* done is accept me unconditionally. And I truly believe they do this because they themselves were shunned for choosing each other and know exactly how it feels to be judged and discriminated against because of whom you love.

I put my arms around her and kiss her on the cheek. "Thank you, Ammi. She's really upset."

"Don't worry too much, chanda. I'm sure her parents will

come around sooner or later. And Chloe can stay here as long as she likes. I will talk to her mother myself and let her know she'll be well taken care of."

"I've never met them, Ammi. I don't know what they'll think of her staying here with us."

"Yes, I understand, Zara, but we can't just let her parents worry, hai na?"

Just then the doorbell rings, and I run to open the door. Chloe has a large backpack slung around her shoulder. Her face is tear-streaked and puffy, and she bursts into tears as soon as she comes in and drops the bag on the floor. I put my arms around her and try to console her. I lead her to the couch in the living room. Ammi follows us and sits next to Chloe.

"Chloe, do you want to talk about it?" Ammi asks gently.

Chloe shakes her head. "Not really. It's just too hard right now."

Ammi nods. "Okay, then, I'll let you girls talk, and I'll make some pizza rolls in case you get hungry. Dinner's going to be a while."

"Do you want to go up to my room?" I ask.

Chloe nods through her tears, and I gently take her by the hand to lead her upstairs.

"I can't believe my parents are being so ridiculous. They keep saying that they love me but what I'm doing is wrong and they have to make sure I stay on the right path."

"What the hell does that even mean?"

"They just want me to be 'normal,'" Chloe says. "Basically, just don't be a lesbian. As if I woke up one morning and decided that this would be a fun thing to try out."

"They really have no clue, do they?"

Chloe shakes her head.

"Honestly, I don't even know how that's possible these days. I

164

mean, they're not hermits, but they act like we're living in the Middle Ages."

I don't know what to say that won't sound trite, so I put my arm around her and pull her close. She leans into me and sighs deeply.

"I just wanted to get away, you know. I'm so tired of the way they make me feel." She starts sobbing again. "Like there's something wrong with me that needs to be fixed."

"I'm so sorry, Chloe. I wish there was something I could do to make this better." I stroke her hair, which smells of ocean and sunshine.

"I just want my parents to stop using God as an excuse and admit that they're the ones who have a problem with me being gay." Chloe balls her hands into fists. "It makes me so angry that I just want to scream at them."

I get how she feels. It's just like when our school refused to let us have a GSA club. After we got hundreds of signatures and the board members were called out for discrimination, they came up with a clever solution. They banned all clubs from being active at school. They were so determined to stop us that they shut everyone down. That's when I realized that things here weren't all that different than they were in Pakistan or any other Muslim country.

But right now, I need to focus on Chloe and make sure she's okay.

"Okay, Chloe," I say in my best take-charge voice. "We can talk more about this tomorrow, and we'll figure out what to do. But for tonight, I say lots of ice cream and movies."

She gives me a tremulous smile and hugs me.

"I'm so glad I have you, Zara," she says, tears welling up in her eyes again, and I hug her back tightly. I hate her parents for hurting her, but I'm determined to help her get through to them.

CHAPTER THIRTY-FOUR

Ammi is getting off the phone just as Chloe and I walk in the front door after school a few days later.

"That was your mom, Chloe," she says. "She really wants you to come home."

Chloe's face falls. It's been three days, and a lot of phone calls between her mom and mine, since Chloe came over to stay with us.

"I'm sorry if I've been here for too long," Chloe starts, but Ammi interrupts her.

"No, no, that's not what I meant at all, Chloe. You're welcome to stay as long as you like. But I do think you should talk to your mom because she's really upset."

"I guess I should call her back, then," Chloe says hesitantly, pulling out her cell phone. Ammi and I go to the kitchen to give her some privacy.

"Do you think her parents will ever understand?" I ask Ammi.

She puts the kettle on for tea and pulls out a dish of kheer from the fridge.

"I'm not sure, beta. But I do know they have to sort it out."

"What did she say to you about all this? I don't think Chloe should have to go back home just because her mom's upset."

"No, of course not," Ammi says. She spoons some kheer into a glass bowl for me and slides it over. "But this is not a permanent solution either."

I push away the bowl of kheer. I have no appetite for dessert while my girlfriend is struggling with her family.

"They need to open their minds. Why should she have to feel bad about herself just because they're blind to the real world?"

"Zara, believe me when I tell you that Chloe's parents are not the most narrow-minded people you'll come across."

"I know, Ammi. I'm not stupid. But still, in this day and age it's just ridiculous."

"Yes, it is. But, Zara, for many people this is still something that goes against their core beliefs," Ammi says. "And I'm not saying it's justified in any way. But it's still real and Chloe will have to face it if she wants to have a relationship with her parents."

Abbu walks in just then. "Everything all right? What are we talking about?"

My parents are so attuned to each other's moods it's uncanny, but #relationshipgoals.

"Chloe's talking to her mom," Ammi says.

Abbu frowns. "I hope they work it out," he says.

"Her mom says she's been talking to their priest," Ammi says.

I roll my eyes. I really don't think talking to their priest will help. Or I don't know, maybe he's super progressive.

"That's like us going and talking to the imam about Zara," Abbu says with a hollow laugh.

Our family doesn't really fit in with the rest of the Muslim community in South Texas. Shireen Khala knows about me because she and Ammi are close. But it's not as if my parents run around town shouting about my bisexuality. Not that they're ashamed of me or anything, but no one in the Muslim community here sits around talking about their kids' sex lives.

Chloe walks into the kitchen just then. Her tearstained face is enough to tell me that the conversation with her mom wasn't easy. We all wait for her to speak.

"Okay, so my mom says she's ready for us to go to family counseling to get through this."

I release a big breath. "That's awesome, Chloe."

Ammi nods too. "This is good news, right?"

"I guess so," Chloe says, smiling for the first time in a long while. "I mean, it's a start at least."

"Good. I really hope things work out," Abbu says. "But remember, you are always welcome in our home."

Chloe's eyes fill with tears, and she hugs both my parents. Then we go upstairs to pack up her things.

"Will you be okay?" I ask, reaching for her hand.

"I think so." Chloe dabs her eyes with a tissue. "Mom sounded pretty upset when I talked to her."

"Maybe she realizes that she could lose you."

She shrugs. "All I can do is try to get through to them. I'm not going to let them make me feel awful about myself again."

I squeeze her shoulders. "If you do, promise me you'll come straight here."

She takes my face in her hands and kisses me gently.

"Thanks for everything, Zara."

I'm sad that she won't be staying with us anymore but also happy that her family would try to work things out.

● ● ●

The next day at school, I'm walking past the library to find a quiet spot for lunch. I haven't really been hanging out with Priya and Nick a lot since the day we went to Victoria. Part of me is still pissed at them for not understanding that I needed to hold on to my anger. But another part of me really misses my best friends. I turn the corner and see Nick and Priya sitting at our usual lunch spot. They're talking, heads bent close together, and Nick must have said something funny because Priya throws back her head and laughs. That's when she sees me, and a look flashes across her face. It's just for a second and then it's gone, but I swear it looked like guilt. Nick follows her gaze, and when he sees me, he hesitates for a millisecond and then waves me over. I walk over to them, but I can't help feeling like I'm crashing a private party.

"Hey," I say, standing awkwardly in front of them.

"Hey," Nick says.

"Where've you been?" Priya says. "You always disappear right after class."

"Yeah, sorry, I've just been dealing with some stuff." As soon as I say it, I feel ridiculous. This is *not* how I talk to Nick and Priya.

"Do you want to talk about it?" Nick says. "Or are you still mad at us?"

Trust him to get straight to the point.

"No." I sigh and sink down beside him. "Everything just sucks."

"Uncle's okay, right?" he says. "Dad went to see him yesterday. He said he's doing much better."

"Did he tell him that we might be moving back?"

"Back where?" Priya says.

"To Pakistan."

"What? Why?" Nick sits up straight. "What're you talking about?"

I tell them all about the problem with our green card application and Abbu's trespassing plea.

"That's ridiculous," Nick says. He's fuming. "I mean, y'all have been waiting for eight years."

"There has to be some other way," Priya says.

I shake my head. "Nothing's for sure yet," I say. "But I can tell that my parents are done with this place. They just don't feel safe here anymore."

"I don't blame them," Priya says. "But you're planning to go away to college anyway, right?"

"Can't they stay until you leave?" Nick asks.

"Abbu's work visa expires in a couple of months," I say. "If he doesn't get it renewed, my dependent status becomes invalid. So I'll have to leave the country before then."

"This is really bad," Priya says. "You've only been there once or twice since you moved here, right?"

I nod. "Twice. It's been a few years, and I loved it. But I don't know if I want to live there permanently."

"What does Chloe say?" Nick asks.

"I haven't told her," I say quietly.

The bell rings for next period, and we all rush off to our respective classes. But I can't focus on English because my mind is on the difficult conversation I need to have with Chloe.

CHAPTER THIRTY-FIVE

I meet Chloe at Scoopz. We haven't come here for some time, and I feel that sugar is always great when delivering bad news. We get our usual, mango with sour gummies.

As we're waiting to be rung up, I ask her how things are going with her parents. We've texted, but it's important to get a face-to-face answer.

"I guess I made my point," she says, picking a gummy worm from our bowl and popping it into her mouth. "But they keep making theirs too, mostly through silence."

"Are you all still going to see a counselor?" I ask.

She nods. "Next week—that's the first appointment she had. So I think we'll be walking on eggshells until then."

"Well, you said you felt like you were doing that anyway, right?" I say. "At least you're all there now."

"How're your parents holding up?" she asks as soon as we're sitting. "I know it's only been a day, but I miss them."

"They're okay. As best as they can be, under the circumstances, I guess."

"Did something else happen?"

I tell her what my parents said about moving back, without really giving the timeline of when they said it. Chloe gets quiet, and I reach over to take her hand.

"Do you have to go too?" she asks.

"I can't stay in the country without them."

Like Nick and Priya, she asks about college, and I explain that my status is dependent on my dad's work visa for now.

"Wow, I had no idea," she says. "I guess I just assumed you were born here."

"No, I came here with my parents when I was three. I wish I could just wait until after we graduate," I say. "But I'm not sure my dad's work permit will get renewed if he's unable to practice and if he has a conviction on his record, even if it's a misdemeanor."

"I can't believe it. It's so unfair." Her eyes are shining, and she tightens her grip on my hand.

"Look, nothing's for sure yet, but I just wanted to tell you where things stand right now."

"I'm so glad you did," she says. "You shouldn't have to deal with all this on your own."

She pulls me close and holds me tight. I don't want to dwell on the fact that I have precious few moments like these left with her, but it's hard not to.

We sit like this for a while, and then the shop is closing and we have to leave. There's a heaviness in our steps as we walk out to my car and I drive her home. We both know that things are changing, and it's beyond our control to do anything about it.

• • •

Over the next few days, things at home are weird. Ammi and Abbu are constantly having these whispered conversations that stop as soon as I enter the room.

I finally confront them about it.

"Have you two made up your minds about going back to Pakistan?" I ask. "Or is it still up for discussion?"

"Zara, beta, why would we make such an important decision without talking to you first?" Abbu says.

"I don't know," I say. "I always see you talking about something, and it feels like you're trying to keep it from me."

"We're just weighing our options and don't want to stress you out," Ammi says.

"Anyway, we've decided to hold off on anything until we find out what is happening with the green card," Abbu says.

"Did Shireen Khala say how long that might take?"

Ammi shakes her head. "All we know is that these things move very slowly."

"We still have four months before my H-1B expires," Abbu says. "By then, I'm sure we'll have something."

• • •

The next day at school, Nick catches up with me in the hallway.

"You're not really going to let this happen, are you?" he says.

"Do you have a better idea? Because if you do, I'd love to hear it."

"Zara, when have you ever just accepted something like this?"

I stop in my tracks and turn to face him, my hands balled into fists by my sides.

"What do you want from me, Nick?"

"I want you to fight. You can't just leave."

"Do you think I *want* to leave? But I don't know what to do!"

"We'll figure it out together," he says. "But please don't give up."

"Who said anything about giving up?" I say. "I'm going to figure something out."

Priya's suggested that I talk to Ms. Talbot, since she's been involved with immigrant activism before and might know people who can help. I find her in her office and knock on the door.

"Hey, Ms. Talbot, do you have a minute?"

She looks up and smiles when she sees me. "Sure, come on in, Zara. What can I do for you?"

I catch her up on my current situation.

"My goodness, Zara, I had no idea," she says. "I'm so sorry. Your family has had to deal with so much already. Now you might not even get your green cards after all these years? Unbelievable."

"Honestly, I don't even know what to feel." I let out a big sigh. "I can't believe I've worked so hard for nothing."

"What do you mean? You can still get into college, right?"

I shake my head.

"But what about a student visa?" Ms. Talbot says. "Can't you just apply for that?"

"I can. But it's complicated. I'd have to apply from my home country, so I'd have to wait until I'm back in Pakistan, and even if I do that, there are limited seats available for international students. Plus, the tuition is so much higher. I could never afford it."

Ms. Talbot puts a comforting hand on my shoulder.

"Look, Zara, I know everything seems really bleak now, but you can't give up hope. There's always a way."

"I really hope so," I say.

"Actually, I have an idea," Ms. Talbot says as I turn to walk away. "My wife works with Senator Delgado."

"Susan Delgado? Isn't she the one who formed the subcommittee on immigration and citizenship after all the detentions at the border recently?"

Ms. Talbot smiles. "I didn't realize you knew about that."

"Well, I haven't been getting a lot of sleep lately after . . . you know. So I've had a lot of time to do my own research."

"Anyway, let me talk to her and see if we can figure something out."

CHAPTER THIRTY-SIX

The next afternoon, the doorbell rings just as I'm coming down the stairs. I run to open the door and find two people from Abbu's hospital standing outside. It's Dr. Alter, the head of Abbu's hospital, holding a bouquet of flowers alongside Mrs. Christiansen, the hospital's chief of staff, holding a box from S & J Bakery. I invite them in before running up to get Abbu. By the time we come down, Ammi has already brought them glasses of ice-cold lemonade and is chatting with them.

"I'm very happy to see that you're doing so much better," Dr. Alter says to Abbu, taking a bite of the coffee cake that Ammi has put out alongside the kolaches.

"Yes, I'm feeling better every day," Abbu says. "My doctor says I should be ready to come back to work soon."

Mrs. Christiansen and Dr. Alter exchange a look.

"Actually, that's what we're here to talk about today," Mrs. Christiansen says.

"Yes, of course," Abbu says with a nod.

Dr. Alter hesitates. "I'm afraid there's a bit of an issue."

The knot in my stomach is back.

"What kind of an issue?" Abbu says.

"Well, as you know, your H-1B visa is coming up for renewal in four months."

"Yes, and the legal department has informed me that our green card application is in its last stages and about to be approved." Abbu leans forward in his chair. "This will be the last time my H-1B visa will need to be renewed."

"Yes, but there's a problem with that," Mrs. Christiansen says. "Our board has expressed that they are no longer willing to sponsor your work visa, in light of the recent incident."

Abbu's face darkens, and Ammi tenses in her seat.

"You mean when I was shot?" Abbu says, his tone quiet.

"Not exactly," Dr. Alter says. "Iqbal, look, you know I would do anything to have you back at work where you belong."

"But?" Abbu says.

"Benson has connections," Mrs. Christiansen says. "And unfortunately, some of those happen to be on our board. Benson has made this a my-side/your-side thing. And they're on his side."

And there it is. The other shoe has dropped.

"What do you mean exactly?" Ammi finally speaks up, and I hear the tremor in her voice.

"Nilufer, I'm so sorry," Mrs. Christiansen says. They've been on a first-name basis for years. We've been to her kids' baptisms. "I tried, but they're not willing to budge. Our hands are tied. The fact that Iqbal pled guilty made it worse."

"To a Class B misdemeanor!" Ammi says. "That's the same as possession of an ounce of marijuana. Or a first drunk-driving offense. Or failure to pay child support. Are you saying that if we looked at your staff, we wouldn't find people who have Class B misdemeanor convictions?"

"Our green card application will not go through," Abbu says, almost to himself. "After all these years. And we were so close."

"How can they do this?" Ammi says. Abbu puts his hand on her forearm and squeezes gently.

"I'm so sorry," Mrs. Christiansen says. "But it's a really bad situation. Things are so delicate these days, you know. If we lose the financial support of our board, there will be no hospital. It's unfortunately as simple as that."

"So, what happens now?" I've found my voice again.

"I will personally write you the best possible recommendation," Dr. Alter says to Abbu.

But we're not fooled. We know that won't be enough.

The two of them leave after apologizing a few more times. Although I don't doubt the sincerity of their words, I'm not sure that they fully comprehend the chaos they have thrown us into.

We sit in silence after they leave, each of us lost in our own troubled thoughts. I'm not sure the whole impact of what they said has sunk in yet.

"Iqbal, what's going to happen now?" Ammi says. "If they don't renew your visa . . ." Her voice trails off.

"Can't Abbu get a different job?" I ask.

"No, beta, the hospital sponsored my green card application, so even if I get another job, that employer will have to be willing to sponsor me and then we'll have to start the whole process all over again."

"But how is this fair?" I say. "You're the victim here. You didn't do anything wrong."

"I know, Zara," Abbu says patiently. "As Dr. Alter said, it's a matter of sides. And in this case, we're on the wrong side."

"What are we supposed to do now?" I ask.

"First let's call Shireen and see what she thinks," Abbu says.

Ammi goes off to make the call. I scoot my chair closer to Abbu.

"How can they do this, Abbu? After knowing you and working with you for all these years."

"I know, beta." Abbu gently strokes the top of my head. "You don't worry about all this. Just keep your focus on school. We'll figure something out."

I know Abbu always wants to shield me from the harsh realities of life, but I have a feeling this is something he can't fix.

CHAPTER THIRTY-SEVEN

The next evening, Ammi, Abbu, and I sit around the dining table for an early dinner of turkey sandwiches and salad.

"Zara, we want to talk to you about something," Abbu says. "But you have to promise to stay calm and hear us out."

In the history of conversations, has that line ever worked?

"What is it?" I say, trying to ignore the knot in my stomach.

"You know that Abbu and I were talking about this before," Ammi says. "And then it seemed for a bit that things might be all right after all."

"But now, after what happened yesterday, we've decided that we want to leave," Abbu says.

"I don't understand," I say. "What happened to staying and fighting?"

"We're tired, Zara," Ammi says. "We've been fighting for years."

"But now we just don't want to stay where we're not welcome," Abbu says. "Look at everything that's happened. It's not safe for us anymore."

"We think it's better if we just go back home," Ammi says. "Abbu can start his own practice there. And we'll be with our families."

Home. Such a loaded word. It's strange to think that perhaps for my parents this has never really been home. Even though they chose to come here and built a good life, to them home will probably always mean Pakistan, where they grew up surrounded by extended family and people who looked like them, where they didn't have to explain their existence constantly. But to me, Corpus is home. It's where all my memories were born even though I wasn't.

"But what about me?" I say.

"Beta, there are excellent colleges in Karachi also, you know," Ammi says. "And who knows what opportunities you'll have in the future? Maybe you'll be able to come back one day."

I'm speechless. My brain can't process the words I'm hearing right now.

"But this is home," I finally say.

Ammi gives a bitter laugh. "What home? Where you can get shot in someone's driveway? Where we have to be scared all the time because of what we believe?"

"Zara, you don't understand how much we've sacrificed so that you can have a better future," Abbu says. "At least, that's what we thought we were giving you. But now I'm not so sure anymore. Look at how things are for Muslims in this country. We're all being punished for crimes committed by people who are nothing like us. But we all have to pay the price. Constantly."

"And, beta, I'm tired of worrying every time you step out the door," Ammi says. "You aren't even safe in school here. What will happen when you go away to college? Things seem to be getting worse for us every day. I don't know how much longer I can take it."

"What if I don't want to go?" I say. "What if there is a way to stay?"

"I don't know how that's going to be possible," Abbu says. "But why would you want to stay when it's clear that they don't want us here?"

"Not everyone is like that, Abbu," I protest. "And you know that. When I went to that rally in Victoria, there were so many people who were there to support us."

"Beta, it takes a lot more than joining one march to change the way things are," Abbu says. "Policies need to be changed as well as people's attitudes."

"Look how quickly the hospital administration turned its back on almost fourteen years of your father's work," Ammi says. "All his dedication and the good he's done. Wiped out just like that without a second thought. Just because of one racist person and his connections. What about standing up for us? But no, it's much easier just to get rid of us."

"I agree with everything you're saying," I say. "But my whole life is here. And my whole identity is here. You don't know how much I appreciate how accepting you are of me being bisexual. I can't be openly queer in Pakistan. I know there have been some positive changes for the LGBTQ+ community there, but there's still a long way to go before people can come out freely and safely. And I refuse to live in any place where I have to hide who I am."

"Look, beta," Abbu says. "We won't force you to do anything. If you want to try and find a way to stay, we will support you however we can. But Ammi and I cannot stay here any longer."

There's nothing left to say. They've made up their minds, and now it's up to me to decide what I want my future to look like. I go up and get ready for bed, but sleep is impossible. Instead, I consider my options.

If I go back to Pakistan with my parents, I'll be a stranger in my own land. I'll be surrounded by people, cousins, and neighbors who will only deepen my longing to be with Nick, Chloe, and Priya, the people who share my memories, who are a real part of my life, not faces in pictures and videos sent of weddings and births and celebrations, people who share my blood but whose relationship with me I can barely keep track of.

I know that my parents don't feel safe here anymore. I am proud to be a Muslim woman. I am proud of my Pakistani culture. And I'm proud to be queer. I should not have to feel unsafe because of any of those parts of my identity, wherever I live. I have a right, just like anyone else, to live without constantly looking over my shoulder and watching my words or my actions. I deserve the dignity to exist as I am. In a perfect world I would be able to do just that. But I'm not so naive that I think the world is perfect.

I have two paths in front of me. One leads me back to Pakistan, where I'm sure I can build a new life and still stay in touch with my friends. I can still get my education and go to law school. After all, Pakistan has plenty of powerful and highly educated women. Maybe one day I might even find my way back here. But the fact remains that I'll have been driven out of here through no fault of my own. So, I choose the other path. I choose to fight. I have to try.

My confidence bolstered, I get out of bed and open my laptop. Two hours and many articles later, I have come up with nothing. There's simply no precedent for a case like ours. We're not undocumented; we're not being deported. Visa applications get rejected all the time. That's all that's really happening to us. But it's the principle of the thing. How is it that after my father was the victim of a racist attack and almost died, we are the ones who are told to leave and are having our entire lives turned upside down? How is this fair?

How is this happening?

CHAPTER THIRTY-EIGHT

I call Shireen Khala as soon as I think she might be awake on a Saturday morning, and we arrange to meet at a coffee shop. Now that my parents have told me how they feel, I don't want to discuss all this in front of them anymore.

We get right down to it as soon as we've exchanged hugs and ordered our coffees.

"So, I've made some calls and it looks like your parents have no choice but to leave the country before your father's visa expires," she says. "Of course, Iqbal Bhai could look for another job and try to get sponsored again."

"I don't think they have any interest in going through all this again," I say with a sigh. "They're speaking of going back for good."

"What? When did they decide this?" Shireen Khala says. "I just talked with them yesterday."

"They told me last night," I say. "It sounds like they've been considering it for some time."

"I can't say I blame them," Shireen Khala says. "After what they've been through, I can't imagine that I'd want to stay either."

"I know and I get it too, but . . ." My voice trails off.

Shireen Khala puts down her coffee cup. "I wish I had better news," she says.

"Thank you for looking into it," I say. "I really appreciate it."

"I wish I could do more," she says. "But I want to discuss your options as well. It looks like you can request to change to a student visa. The only problem is that you'd be considered an international student."

"Exactly. And there's no way I can afford that kind of tuition. I'd have to try and get a scholarship or something. I can't expect Abbu and Ammi to support me if they're earning in rupees. It'll be way too much."

"But it is the only feasible option for now," she says. "Although I must warn you that it's highly unlikely that it will go through in the next four months, so you'll still have to leave the country and wait until you have your student visa in order to reenter."

My heart sinks. I was really hoping she would have some better news. But there was nothing more she could do.

"I wish Ammi and Abbu wouldn't give up so easily," I say once we've gotten refills.

"I know it might seem like that to you, Zara," Shireen Khala says. "But I don't really think they're giving up."

"What do you mean?"

"Well, they came here for you. To give you a better life, more opportunities."

"But they've had a good life too."

"Yes, of course," she says. "But have you considered what they've given up?"

"I mean, yes, I know, but I always thought it's what they wanted."

"Zara, think about it," she says. "Imagine leaving behind

everything you know, everything that is home, for you to go and start a life somewhere far away. Without your support system or anything familiar. Even if you know you're doing it for a good reason, it's still incredibly difficult."

She's given me a lot to think about, so after we're done, I drive back home to grab Zorro and take him for a walk. We go along the water as usual, the sound of the waves crashing against the shore lulling me into a state of calm. I feel like I'm at war with myself. One part of me feels the same way my parents do, angry at this country that seems to be rejecting me after offering the false promise of home. I long to be with people who accept me as I am, to be around family who lives and talks and celebrates like I do. But at the same time, I don't believe I'll fit in completely in Pakistan either, after all these years of living here. And it isn't anything singular; it's a multitude of small things that will set me apart: the way I talk and eat and move all will mark me as an outsider. Sure, those things will slowly change over time. I notice it when I watch my parents in old home videos. Their accents, their body language, all of those have changed, almost imperceptibly over the years.

The question is: Did they want these changes? Or did they just happen anyway?

• • •

Ms. Talbot calls me into her office on Monday.

"Zara, I have some good news," she says to me when I'm sitting across from her.

"I could really use some good news."

"Sylvia told me she'll talk to the senator about your situation and see if she can help in any way."

I jump up. "Oh my God, really? That would be amazing.

Thank you so much." I rush over to hug her and then step back awkwardly.

"I'm glad I could help," she says with a smile. "Of course, there's no guarantee that the senator will be able to do anything, but it's a start."

"You have no idea how much this means to me, Ms. Talbot," I say. "And please thank your wife for me too."

"I will. And I'll let you know as soon as I hear something."

CHAPTER THIRTY-NINE

"So, did she say what she could do?" Nick takes a sip of his chocolate milkshake. We're at La Paletera and I've just finished telling him what Ms. Talbot said.

"No, her wife will talk about it with the senator and hopefully she can help." I take a long sip of my frozen cappuccino and regret it immediately when the brain freeze hits.

"Have you told Chloe yet?" Nick asks.

"No, I haven't had a chance to tell her yet," I say.

"So, you're telling me first?" Nick gives me a smug smile before taking another sip.

"Well, I was craving a cappuccino freeze and you happened to be available," I say, trying hard not to smile. "That's the only reason, so you don't have to feel so special."

"Whatever you say," he says.

I mutter things to myself that I wouldn't say out loud in public, ignoring his stupid grin.

• • •

I tell Chloe later that night when I'm in bed.

"That's so great," she says. "I'm so glad you might finally

be getting somewhere with your visas. I hope the senator is able to pull some strings so your family can stay."

"I know, me too," I say. "After my parents told me they wanted to leave, I was almost ready to give up."

"Don't say that, Zara."

"Part of me sort of agrees with what they said." I let out a deep sigh. "You know, I was thinking about what my life would be like if I really left."

Chloe is silent for a bit, and the steady sound of her breathing is the only thing I can hear. It's calming, somehow.

"Am I in the picture in that version of your life?" she finally asks. I realize that I haven't really considered how she'll deal with all of this.

"I don't even know if *I'm* there, to be honest. It doesn't feel real." I'm glad that I can be completely open with her, even if it's hard to talk about.

"I can't even imagine how weird this all must be for you," she says.

"Anyway, enough about me," I tell her. "How was the therapist? I want details."

"I don't know . . . it was like the therapist was on my side, which I wasn't expecting," she says, and I can almost hear a smile in her voice. "I don't think my parents were expecting it either. It was like she presented it as a problem they were having, not a problem I was having."

"That's so great. At least you don't have to feel like it's just you against them all the time."

"Exactly. And instead of stomping out of the room, my parents listened. To be honest, I think my father would've happily stomped out of the room. But my mother's now the one in charge. Like, if it were the Supreme Court, she'd be the swing vote."

We explore this feeling some more, and when I hang up, I feel as close to Chloe as I've ever felt. But as I drift off to sleep, a sliver of guilt nags at me. I go back to her question and wonder, *What does the picture of my new life look like . . . and is she in it?*

The question stays with me throughout the following day as I try to keep my mind on my schoolwork, something that is getting increasingly more difficult to do. If I'm not trying to figure out my feelings for Chloe, then I'm worrying about whether I will even be here after four months.

In the meantime, Shireen Khala has convinced Ammi and Abbu to appeal the denial of Abbu's H-1B renewal. She says that the negotiations about Mr. Benson's case are still happening, and that if he ends up pleading guilty to get a reduced sentence, then that could change some of the board members' feelings. The trial isn't scheduled for months, but the prosecutor has told Shireen Khala that he senses their side wants to settle sooner rather than later, "to get this behind them." I don't want them to be able to get it behind them, but I would love a resolution that helped our argument. If the hospital board reconsiders, then we'll be back on track for our green cards. For the first time in days, I feel it's possible—slightly possible—that we won't have to leave.

• • •

Chloe comes over to hang out after school the next day, and since Ammi has taken Abbu to physical therapy, we have the whole house to ourselves. We cuddle on the couch, and soon Chloe's lips are on mine and I'm lost in the warmth of her touch. It's been a while since we've been together like this, and with everything that's happened in the last couple of months, I feel like we haven't really had a chance to ease into our relationship. This whole thing with Tyler happened so soon after the first time we even went out together, it's as if we were on pause while it was all happening, and now that I know I might have to leave, there's a sense of urgency in all our interactions.

So, it's nice to have a moment like this when we're just kissing and the rest of the world fades away. But the sadness always comes back, pushing all the happy thoughts to the side.

"Are you okay?" she asks.

"Yeah, it's just, I can't figure out what I'm going to do."

"Okay, so let's talk about it," Chloe says.

I sit back all the way, pushing my head against the cushion. "I guess with so much up in the air, it's hard to make any decisions."

"I totally get that," she says. "I wish I could do something to help. I feel so useless."

I take her hand. "Please don't say that. You're here for me, and that's what matters."

I put my head on her lap, and she runs her fingers through my hair. A calm settles over me, and I lift my head up just enough to meet her lips.

For the next little while, nothing comes between us. We only jump apart when we hear Ammi's car pull into the driveway.

CHAPTER FORTY

Ms. Talbot calls me on Friday to tell me that Senator Delgado's assistant can see me on Monday at four in the afternoon.

"That's great, Ms. Talbot!" I say. "Thank you so much again."

"Of course," she replies. "I hope she can help. Please let me know how it goes."

"For sure. I really hope there's something we can do."

• • •

On Monday, Shireen Khala picks me up for the appointment. We drive to city hall, where the meeting is scheduled, and my stomach is doing somersaults as we take the elevator up to the tenth floor. If the senator's assistant doesn't think there's anything she can do, then I'm back to square one. We step off the elevator into a brightly lit lobby and approach the reception.

The man behind the desk looks up at me expectantly.

"I'm here to see Ms. Anderson," I say.

"Name?" he asks, looking down at his computer.

"Zara Hossain."

"Please have a seat," he says, not looking away from his

screen. "Ms. Anderson will be with you when she's ready."

Shireen Khala and I grab a couple of seats near the reception desk. It's fairly empty in here, probably because it's close to the end of day. I look around while we wait, wondering what it might be like to work in a place like this one day.

"Just remember to tell her everything," Shireen Khala tells me in a low voice. "Especially about your volunteer history and your goals for your future."

I nod. "I will."

I hear my name, and we both stand and walk over to where the receptionist is pointing. A door to my right opens, and a woman steps out. She seems to be in her thirties, dressed formally in a pantsuit with her dark blond hair in a severe bun. The brown frames of her glasses add to the seriousness of her look, but a smile brightens her face as she holds out her hand.

"Zara, I'm Vanessa Anderson. It's very nice to meet you."

After introductions are out of the way, the three of us sit in her office with cups of coffee on the table in front of us.

"Thank you so much for taking the time to meet with me," I say.

"Oh, it's my pleasure," she says. "Sylvia spoke very highly of you."

I'll have to remember to bring Ms. Talbot's wife a thank-you gift for talking me up.

I start at the beginning and tell Ms. Anderson everything that's happened. When I'm done, she takes a deep breath.

"That's a very difficult thing to go through, Zara," she says. "I'm happy to hear that your father is doing better, but this situation is simply not right."

"Do you think there's any way they can remain in the

country?" Shireen Khala asks. "Zara's future is at stake, and she's worked so hard."

"Well, there's always something," Ms. Anderson tells us. "The problem is finding the solution in time before Dr. Hossain's work visa expires."

"I only have four months," I say. "I won't even be here long enough to graduate high school. I'll have to leave before the school year ends."

"Here's what we're going to do," Ms. Anderson says. "I'm going to pass this on to Senator Delgado. Hopefully this is something that she'll be willing to take on. But, Zara, I have to warn you, I cannot guarantee anything."

"Of course. I understand," I say quickly.

"But what I can promise you is that I will do everything I can to make sure that we explore any and all options." She smiles gently at me. "We wouldn't want to lose a driven, community-minded, and intelligent young woman like you."

A blush creeps into my face at her praise as she stands to signal the end of our meeting.

"I really appreciate this, Ms. Anderson," I say as we're leaving. There's spring in my step as we walk out because I just have this feeling that something good will come out of this meeting.

• • •

"Zara, come down for dinner, please."

Ammi has made khichdi, which is just the comfort food I'm craving. Usually she makes it when one of us is having tummy troubles because the one-pot rice-and-lentil dish is easy to digest. But today she's spiced it up with green chilies and garnished it with crispy fried onions. And there's mango achaar to go with it. Yum. I liberally add the spicy pickle to my khichdi and start to eat.

"Zara, have you heard anything more from the senator's assistant you went to see the other day?" Abbu asks.

"No, not yet, but I'm sure she's very busy," I say.

"Beta, I don't want you to get your hopes too high," Ammi says. "As it is, these things take so long, but our case is particularly difficult."

"So what should I do, Ammi? I can't just give up. I have to at least try."

"Yes, baba, try," Abbu says placatingly, "but you should also have a backup plan, hai na?"

Ammi spoons some more khichdi onto my plate. "If you end up coming back to Karachi with us, you will have to apply for colleges there too."

While they'd mentioned going to college in Pakistan, the fact that I'd have to apply hadn't even entered my mind. But she's right. I can't just do nothing if I have to live there.

"I'll ask Fahim Mama to gather some information and send it to us," Ammi says.

"Can you imagine living there again after all these years?" I ask.

Ammi and Abbu look at each other. Suddenly I'm not sure if I want to hear their answer, but it's too late now.

"Actually, I never wanted to come here in the first place," Ammi says. "But your father thought that you would have more opportunities here."

"Well, I wasn't wrong, hai na, Nilufer? She would have had a lot of opportunities if it hadn't been for that boy and his father."

Abbu hasn't talked about the shooting a single time since he woke up from his coma, other than whatever he said to the police. He's refused to see a therapist and has asked us not to bring it up again. But I can only imagine how much pain and anger is festering inside him. For all his progressive ways of thinking, Abbu still thinks that talking to someone about his mental well-being is a sign of weakness.

I'm starting to think that maybe it is better for him to go back and get a fresh start while being surrounded by his extended family.

Ammi continues the conversation. "No, not wrong, Iqbal, but think about all we missed," she says. "Our siblings have children we've never met, some of our relatives have died, and we never got a chance to say goodbye. So many words were said years ago, and because we left, we never got a chance to repair the damage."

"You're saying all this now because of what happened," Abbu says. "Otherwise you were perfectly happy in your life here."

"Or maybe I convinced myself that I was happy without my parents and my brother and all my childhood friends," Ammi says. "People who really know me, who understand where I come from."

"What about Isabella and Shireen?" Abbu says.

"Iqbal, now you're being ridiculous. Of course, I cherish Isabella and Shireen. But I'm just saying, when I was younger, my cousins and I used to talk about our kids playing together and growing up side by side. And now we barely know who their kids are."

Abbu lets out a deep sigh. "I know, Nilufer. We both made sacrifices, but that's what you have to do when you want to have a better life."

"That's just what I'm saying. What was wrong with our lives before we came here?"

"Nothing was wrong. But why not try to have more if you can?"

They fall silent after that, and I sit at the table wondering if everything I thought about them was a lie. Or a half-truth. And I feel responsible for all of it, because if it hadn't been for me, maybe they would have been perfectly content staying home in Karachi.

I help clean up and leave them to their uncomfortable silence to go to my room. I finish up the rest of my math worksheet, but my mind keeps wandering to the dinner conversation.

How would I feel if I had to go back? What would I miss the most in my day-to-day life? Going for milkshakes and movies whenever I felt like it? Being free to dress however I want? I may not have lived there for years, but I've gleaned enough from conversations to know that it's different over there, especially for women. I won't have the kind of freedom I enjoy here. But there are certain things that I'll never get here. Like that sense of belonging where you just fit in with everyone and you're part of a larger family and it won't always just be the three of you. I have so many cousins, a lot of them my age, and it'll be like I have my own siblings, something I've wished for all my life.

But then I'll never get to hang with Nick and Priya again. And what about Chloe? I definitely wouldn't feel safe coming out to everyone there. I highly doubt that the rest of my family will be as open-minded about my bisexuality as my parents are.

How many people will my parents have to fight with on my behalf?

And then who will they have left if they alienate everyone in their family?

What choices will I really have?

CHAPTER FORTY-ONE

I still haven't heard anything from Ms. Anderson, and I'm slowly losing hope. I try to read articles about immigration issues because I'm obsessed with numbers and percentages of people in similar situations.

I read an article that says children of immigrants often age out of the green card process when they turn twenty-one. So even if we hadn't been in this mess with Abbu's work visa, there was a very good chance that I might've had to start the application process from scratch if we didn't get our green cards in three years. It's already been eight, and of course now we're out of the running. But the idea that there's no system in place to safeguard children who legally came to this country with their immigrant parents as infants and who might be deported because there's such a backlog of pending applications just blows my mind.

My parents often talk about how the US need for high-skilled workers, many from South Asia, outweighs the local supply, and it doesn't make sense to me. As a doctor, my father's skills were in high demand when my parents moved here with me fourteen years ago. That's why the hospital agreed to sponsor his green card application swiftly and why they were paying for all legal services. But why make it so hard for people to actually remain in the country, especially after the employers have invested so much time and money into training and honing the skills of the people who come here? I read that there's a minimum seven-year wait for applicants from South Asian countries. With the current backlog, this could take much longer.

I find articles that talk about the dire need for immigration reform, and Susan Delgado's name keeps popping up. Immigration reform is one of the issues of her upcoming presidential campaign. It seems like fate has led me to her office to meet with her assistant. Maybe our case can be something she'll use as an example of how badly the current system needs to be revamped. I wonder if she's had a chance to look into it.

● ● ●

I stand in front of my full-length mirror and study my reflection. I'm wearing a brand-new churidaar suit, a turquoise-and-silver embroidered set with matching bangles and silver dangly earrings. We're driving to San Antonio to attend a cultural event organized by the Pakistani Association where there are stalls selling everything from food to glass bangles to embroidered household items. It's also a chance to socialize because almost everyone comes out to enjoy traditional Pakistani snacks and entertainment. I invited Chloe, and she's brimming with excitement as she plays with the thin silver bangles I gave her. She's wearing one of my suits, a light pink one with silver sequins dotted all over, and she looks radiant. We meet up with Nick and Priya, who also drove up, and browse a few more stalls before stopping for chaat. I love the tartness of the chaat masala mixed in with guavas and apples, and I'm glad to see that Chloe is enjoying it too. We stop at a stall selling gorgeous cushion covers embroidered with little pieces of glass. I buy a matching set for Ammi, even though a nagging voice in my head reminds me that she'll be able to buy all this in Karachi herself very soon. But I choose to ignore this voice because I need a break, just for today, to forget about everything. An announcement reminds us that the Nazia Hassan tribute will begin soon. Ammi and Abbu introduced me to her music when we watched *Qurbani*, me for the first time and my parents probably for the fiftieth. She sang one of the most popular songs in the movie, and I instantly fell in love with it. I'm probably the only teen in the entire state of Texas who loves the song that ushered the disco era into Bollywood. "Aap Jaisa Koi" was my favorite, but once my parents realized I liked it, they wasted no time pulling out her entire album, on cassette tape.

When I was eleven or twelve, it wouldn't be at all unusual to find me sitting next to Ammi's old tape deck listening to Nazia's songs. The tape deck doesn't work anymore, but every now and then, I'll find one of her songs on YouTube and relive my glory days as a preteen.

Judging by the crowd gathered by the main stage, it's clear that I'm not the only one with a taste for old people music. The young Pakistani singer who gets onstage flawlessly belts out one of my other Nazia faves, "Disco Deewane." This is exactly what I needed today. My friends and I dance along as the band plays a whole set. Afterward we go and find a stall that sells kulfi. The cardamom-flavored ice cream is perfect for this hot afternoon.

In the evening, there's a performance by a band made up entirely of aunties and uncles, and it's giving me life. They sing old Bollywood songs by Mohammed Rafi and Lata Mangeshkar, and it's the best. I also spy my parents on the other side of the crowd dancing away to the music, and it makes me smile to see them so carefree after a long time. Of course, the evening wouldn't be complete without running into Zareen Aunty, who passes by and throws me a murderous look just as I'm getting another plate of mango slices covered in salt and chili powder. I know I should ignore her, but at the last minute, I change my mind and flash a wicked smile in her direction. I don't wait around to see her reaction, making my way to the main entrance, where my parents said they would wait for me.

"Uff, that Nazia Hassan tribute was too good," Ammi says as she's driving us home.

"I had such a great time," I say. "That singer was amazing."

"What about the final performance?" Ammi asks. "Did you like it?"

"It was the best. Abbu, why didn't you join the group? Last year, you said you were too busy, but you could have joined them this time."

"Beta, I'm hardly in the right state of mind to focus on something like that," Abbu says.

He's right, I guess. We've been through so much these past few months, it feels like we haven't done anything fun for ages. My heart is heavy when I remember just a few months back, when Chloe was with all of us and Abbu sang for us. That seems like ages ago, in a time when life was normal and the biggest thing I had to worry about was Tyler being a jerk. How did we get here?

CHAPTER FORTY-TWO

Ms. Anderson has left a message to call back when I get home from school a few days later. My heart races with anticipation as I return her call immediately. After I hang up, I run around the house to find my parents. I find them in their bedroom. Abbu is a little tired after his physical therapy session and is resting.

"Ms. Anderson had good news to share. She says Susan Delgado wants to meet with us," I say, slightly out of breath.

"That's great," Ammi says. "When are you going to see her?"

"She wants to see all of us. She said she'd like to talk to us together about everything that happened."

Ammi and Abbu look at each other.

"Isn't it better if you go by yourself so that she can focus on you?" Ammi says. "It might be better than having to help all three of us."

"After all, your situation is different from ours, Zara," Abbu says. "It might be easier just to get yours sorted out."

"But what if she can help all of us? Why won't you even try?"

"Beta, we told you already, we don't want to stay here any longer," Ammi says. "You were always planning to go out of state for college, so you'd be living away from us anyway, right?"

"Yes, but this is different. I'd still get to see you during holidays and stuff."

"So now you'll visit us in Karachi," Abbu says. "It'll be good for you to come there."

"But that's not how it was supposed to be."

"I know, beta," Ammi says patiently. "But this is how it is. If you weren't about to finish high school, of course it would be another matter."

I take a deep breath and try to focus on the fact that Susan Delgado wants to meet with me and possibly try to help. That's what's going to get me through this.

• • •

Three days later, I'm sitting across from her. She seems older than my parents, so maybe in her fifties, a petite woman with dark brown hair and piercing eyes. I've read up about her, and I'm in awe of everything she's accomplished. She comes from humble beginnings and is the daughter of immigrants from Guatemala herself. Years ago, her parents struggled to come to this country and survive, but with hard work and perseverance, they were able to make a life for themselves. Susan put herself through college and law school by working multiple jobs to support herself. After facing her share of discrimination, she finally made it into the House of Representatives, and from there she became a senator.

Although I'm meeting her for the first time, I feel some sort of connection with her. Maybe it's because I think that she understands what it's like to be an outsider no matter how long you've lived somewhere. And I'm certain that she remembers the struggles that many immigrants face. Why else would she be willing to help?

"Ms. Delgado, I'm Zara. Thank you so much for taking the time to see me," I say as soon as I walk in. We're in the green room at the KRIS TV station, where she's doing an interview later. This was the only time she had available.

"It's very nice to meet you, Zara. I'm sorry we couldn't meet under better circumstances, but I understand this matter is of some urgency?"

"Yes, ma'am." I recount the entire sequence of events. She listens intently, interrupting a couple of times for clarification. After I'm done, she leans back in her chair and shakes her head.

"I'm so very sorry for what your family is going through. This is simply unacceptable."

"I feel as if we're being punished for something we didn't even do. It's so unfair."

"I agree completely. And let me tell you, Zara, I will do everything in my power to try and either expedite your green card application or find a way to extend your father's work visa."

I get up and shake her hand.

"Thank you so much again, Ms. Delgado. You have no idea how much this means to me."

"Vanessa will be in touch with you soon."

By the time I get home, I'm floating on a cloud. I want to call Nick and Chloe so badly, but I resist the urge. Maybe when I have actual news. But for now, I'm going to focus my energy on staying positive.

● ● ●

Two weeks pass without a word from Senator Delgado, and the optimism that filled me after our meeting slowly depletes.

My parents have already begun to make arrangements for their move back to Pakistan. I notice Ammi starting to pack some of our stuff up. Nothing we use every day, but things that she's kept stored away in the garage, as well as some framed photos that never made it back up on the wall after the last paint job. There's still so much to be done, but luckily many of the family members over there are helping out.

When the call from Senator Delgado's office finally comes in, her assistant invites my parents and me to share our story alongside her at a rally in San Antonio this weekend, which has been organized by the activist group Citizens for Immigration Reform—many of whom are Dreamers—to raise awareness for the dire state of immigration rights in this country.

"Please say that you'll come to the rally on Saturday," I say to my parents at dinner that evening.

"Of course, beta. We'll come with you," Abbu says. "It's very kind of Senator Delgado to do this for us."

"I don't think people understand just how broken the immigration system is," Ammi says. "Not just for the Dreamers, but also for immigrants like us with company-sponsored visas. We entered the country legally and followed all the rules, but we're still at the mercy of the employers' whims."

"That's exactly why we need to fight back," I say. "So that things will *actually* change."

"You're right, Zara," Abbu says. "We should do what we can so that your generation doesn't have to deal with this."

"So, does that mean you'd consider staying if Senator Delgado can pull this off somehow?" I ask hopefully.

"Did she say what her plan was?" Abbu says.

"Not exactly, but she did say she'd look into getting your work visa renewed and have our green card application expedited."

"I'm not sure even *she* can do that," Ammi says.

"We'll see" is the only response I have to that.

• • •

The moment Senator Delgado takes the stage, the crowd erupts in a triumphant chant. I'm filled with hope as I look around and see so many young people from all backgrounds gathered here to fight for our rights. It's a reminder that not everyone thinks like Tyler and his father, that many people believe immigrants make valuable contributions and are vital to enriching the fabric that this country is made of.

She smiles and waves, waiting for the crowd to quiet down before she begins to speak.

"Hello, everyone, and thank you for coming out today," she says. "I am incredibly heartened to see so many of you here, and I'm hopeful that together we can fight for a better, more inclusive, and just future." She talks about the history of immigration in the US and then about her personal story of how her parents came to this country with nothing to call their own and built a good life for their family. She tells us about her own struggles with poverty, racism, and sexism and how she came to be where she is today. It's all very inspiring, and as I look to my parents, I can see they feel the same way.

Finally, Senator Delgado invites us to join her on the stage. My stomach is in knots, and my parents look quite nervous too. But she soon puts them at ease with her sincerity and kind words. The crowd hangs on every word as Senator Delgado shares our whole story, and judging from the gasps, I can tell that they are shocked by how events unfolded.

"I believe in all of you," the senator says in closing, "and I know that if we work together we can accomplish great things and make this country a safe space for all of us."

As I look out across the crowd, I'm moved to tears by the overwhelming feelings of warmth and love. I'm starting to see a future for me here once again, where just a few weeks ago I couldn't imagine one anymore. A future where I'm a part of this community, in which I can make a real difference for others like me, like my parents.

• • •

The next day, I'm walking to the library when I see Nick and Priya at a table out front, their heads together. They're both talking in hushed voices, and Priya throws back her head to laugh at something Nick says. They don't notice me, and I'm glad because I'm not sure how I feel about this.

That evening, Nick and his parents are over for dinner, and I ask Nick to come out to the backyard with me.

"What's up?" he says, sitting on the swing set Abbu put up when we were little. Nick and I must have played out here a thousand times, taking turns pushing each other and building castles in the sandbox.

"I saw you with Priya today," I say. "By the library." I watch him closely, to see how he reacts.

"So?" he says, nonchalant. "You see us there every day."

"So, is it serious?" Nick is a huge flirt, and if he's just messing around with Priya, she could get hurt. And that would ruin everything. So, I have to make sure he's serious this time. And I have a feeling he is. I've never seen him look at a girl the way he was looking at Priya when she was laughing. It was sweet . . . but Nick's an idiot and I have to make sure he doesn't make a huge mess of things.

He stops swinging. "Would you be upset if I said yes?"

I put my hand on my hip. "Look, I don't have time for games," I say. "Are you going to tell me or not?"

"Okay, fine. Yes."

"Yes, what?" I demand.

He narrows his eyes at me.

"Yes, it's serious," he says.

"Okay."

"What do you mean, *okay*?" he says. "Is that all you're going to say?"

"Well, what else do you want me to say?"

"Like . . . are you okay with me and Priya being together?"

Am I okay with my two closest friends being together? I mean, Priya and I are very close, but it's different with Nick. I can only describe what he means to me in Urdu. He's apna. My own. It's hard to explain. We have history. We've shared scraped knees, afternoons in the backyard pool, long nights where we stayed up to look at the stars when we were little, sleeping in tents Abbu would put up for us. He knows I'm terrified of lizards, and I know he hates corn dogs with a weird passion because they made him sick one time when we were seven. He consoled me in kindergarten when Ashley B. said I couldn't come to her birthday party because people with dirty skin weren't allowed. He's always the first person I want to tell stuff, even now.

But even though I'm scared of what this means for me, in my heart I'm so happy for both of them. But I don't see why I can't torture Nick a little longer. The worried look on his face right now makes it totally worth it.

"Of course I'm okay with it," I say. "I mean, why wouldn't I be?"

"I don't know," he says. "I guess I thought you might be worried that things might change between us and it'll be weird hanging out together."

When I don't say anything, he grabs hold of my hand.

"Look, Zara," he says. "We'll always be tight no matter what happens. We have so much history, and I'm always going to

208

want to tell you stuff. And it'll be perfect now because you know Priya so well, you can tell me how to fix things when I screw up." He grins in that way I can't resist.

"Or you could maybe, you know, not screw up that much."

"Dude," he says, his face all serious. "Have you met me?"

"You're an idiot. I think we should go back inside now so I can tell everyone about you and Priya," I say just before I run back inside.

By the time he follows me, I've already blurted it out, and we basically spend the rest of the evening giving Nick a hard time.

But beneath the jovial banter, my heart hurts because I know this might be one of the last times that I get to be like this with all the people I love. I'm afraid that time is running out.

CHAPTER FORTY-THREE

I'm trying to stay focused on school and on my friends. Chloe and I try to see each other when we can. Priya was relieved when I told her I knew about her and Nick—though when she started to give me the details I had to put on the brakes with a very definitive "Ew, STOP!"

My teachers have no idea that I might be leaving, and I intend to keep it that way. Every now and then, I pass Tyler in the hall or have to pass him something in history class, and he looks like a drowning man. After his suspension, he never caught up on his work and failed enough classes to get kicked off the football team. His friends make it clear they blame me for this, making me dodge dirty looks and racist comments when they know no teachers are around. But Tyler doesn't rise to this. He doesn't rise to anything.

I hope his dad ends up in jail soon. I suspect it'll be better for both of us that way.

• • •

"Ammi," I say at dinner after a particularly awful day at school, "I've been thinking, and I'm wondering if I should come back to Karachi with you and Abbu."

Ammi's face lights up in a way I haven't seen for some time now.

"Beta, I know it'll be a huge adjustment for you, but that would make me so happy."

"I just don't know if it's the best decision for me. For my future."

"You know, before all this happened, I had no plans of ever going back other than just to visit. Abbu and I thought we'd grow old here and watch you have a family, and it was all going to be perfect."

"But now everything's changed," I say. "I know. I've been feeling like that too. I thought things were going to be okay once Abbu got better."

"Sometimes I feel like Allah is trying to tell me something," she says. "That it's time to go back home, reconnect with our friends, our family, our roots. This country doesn't want us."

"I'm just worried about college there. I looked up a few in Karachi, and they don't have the kind of programs I'm interested in."

"But, beta, young people there are going to college every day, *and* they have successful careers after. There may not be as many options, but you can still get a good education. After all, your father and I got our degrees there, and so many of your cousins are too."

"I know," I say. "I have a lot to think about before I can decide."

• • •

The next night is Friday, and Chloe and I have a date. It's a beautiful, starlit evening by the time we exit the movie theater and make our way to Ocean Drive to walk by the water for a bit. There are only a few people out on the pier, mostly couples like us, holding hands.

As the cool breeze comes in gently from the water, I feel an intense sense of regret for everything that I'll be missing if I end up going back to Karachi. Even though Chloe and I have only been going out for a few months, there's a connection between us that's special. Maybe it's because everything that's happened has heightened the intensity of our feelings toward each other, but I can't imagine never seeing her again. It's unlikely that I'll be able to come back, and even more unlikely that Chloe could visit me in Pakistan. And I can't just forget about her and the way she makes me feel.

I have no way of knowing what the future has in store for the two of us, but I don't think I'm willing to risk never finding out what could have been. Because in this moment right here, right now, I feel incredibly close to her. The kind of closeness that doesn't require many words. It's when you feel so comfortable with someone that you just want to be there with them.

I turn to her, lifting a hand to caress her face. Then I kiss her gently.

Here, in the moonlight under the stars, I realize that I'm exactly where I need to be.

"What was that for?" Chloe asks when we come up for air. She's smiling, and her brown eyes reflect the moonlight rippling over the water.

"For being here," I say. "And for being you."

We hold each other, fitting perfectly with each other, my head just under her chin. My eyes well up, inexplicably, because I feel content and happy after a long time.

"What is it, Zara?" Chloe leans back and looks at me with concern. "Why're you crying?"

I shake my head, and a laugh escapes me. "I don't even know. I'm such a mess."

"Do you want to talk about it?" she says, wiping away the tears.

"I guess I'm just overwhelmed, with everything at school and those jerks. It's just never-ending."

"Honestly, I don't know how you handle it," she says. "It's a lot to deal with."

"Lately, I've been thinking that maybe my parents are right. Maybe we should all go back to Pakistan."

She goes really still, and I know exactly why.

"I'm not going to do it," I say quickly. "But I came pretty close. I'm just so tired of feeling that I don't belong here, and it doesn't help that I'm reminded every day."

"You do belong here, Zara," she says. "Don't let morons like Tyler drive you away, because then they get to win. And we can't let them."

"I know. But it's getting really hard."

"You know we're all here for you. We want you to stay because we love you. I love you." She looks away, as if suddenly realizing what she said.

"I love you too," I say softly. "Any time I thought about just leaving and going back, I realized that being here with you, like this, is what I want more than anything else. I want to see you and hold your hand and go out with you whenever we want. And I'd be giving all that up if I leave."

She lowers her head to mine, and for the next few minutes, we're lost in the gentleness of the waves, my worries swept away by the tide. And everything feels right again.

CHAPTER FORTY-FOUR

When I get home from school on Monday, I see a message from Vanessa Anderson asking me to call back urgently. My heart is in my mouth when I make the call.

"Ms. Anderson, this is Zara Hossain calling back. You left a message?"

"Yes, Zara, I'm glad you caught me. I was just about to leave for the day."

"Have you heard something?"

"I'm sorry I don't have better news. Senator Delgado was able to pull some favors and have your family's green card application expedited. Unfortunately, it still won't be done in time before your father's H-1B status expires."

My heart sinks. I'd really gotten my hopes up, and now I know I shouldn't have.

"So how long after that will it be done?" I ask.

"It's complicated," Ms. Anderson says. "It'll only be a short period of time, during which you'll have no legal status, which changes things."

"So, we'd be staying in the country illegally?" I don't like where this is going.

"Well, you will have to leave the country before your visa expires, otherwise it's a whole other situation."

"Okay, so we'll leave. But then how soon before I can come back?"

"You'd have to wait until your green card is approved. Unfortunately, because you'll now have left the country, it will take longer because it has to go through a few additional stages."

What she's telling me is that I still have to leave, and I still have to wait for an unknown period of time before I can come back. It makes no sense to me whatsoever.

"Thank you for letting me know," I say. "And please thank Ms. Delgado for me."

I'm trying to feel grateful that they even tried, but the disappointment is too much. All the frustration and anger erupt in me, and I throw myself on the bed, violent sobs racking my shoulders. I don't know what I'm going to do.

• • •

When my parents come home, my tearstained face and puffy eyes tell them what they need to know. They try to make me feel better, but I'm inconsolable.

"At least in Pakistan you'll be with family, your own blood." Ammi puts her hands on my shoulders. "You'll be wanted."

"Until they find out the truth, Ammi. Then what? What will they say when they find out I'm bisexual, that I'm in love with a girl?"

"Zara, why do they have to know about that? That's your personal life. It's none of their business."

"So, you want me to hide it? Pretend to be someone I'm not just to fit in?" I shake my head. She doesn't get it.

"Zara, beta, I don't know what to tell you. All I know is that you'll never be safe here, where everyone can see that you don't belong. At least in Pakistan you'll blend in."

So, these are my choices. Stay here and know that every moment someone could be targeting me with their hate and racism or go to Pakistan with my parents and blend in. Become invisible. No thank you. I'm not going to let anyone make me feel like I have to run and hide.

"Ammi, you don't understand. It's easy for you and Abbu to decide to go back to Pakistan because for you that is home. You both had entire lives there before you moved to Texas. My entire life, all my memories, are here. How can I just leave it all behind?"

"Beta, Ammi is just worried for your safety," Abbu said. "It's better to make new friends and new memories than to live like this, always scared of who will shoot you or attack you. What kind of a life is that?"

"But, Abbu, your life here was not always like that. You've had so many good years, haven't you?"

"That's true, Zara," he says. "We've had many happy years here. But times have changed, and it seems to only be getting more dangerous with each passing day."

"All the more reason to fight back, Abbu. Otherwise where does it end?"

"Uff Allah, Zara, why do *you* have to be the one fighting against all this? Let other people fight, na. I only have one daughter, and I'd like her not to get hurt."

"I'm not going to get hurt, Ammi. This is my fight too. Why should I let a racist like Tyler dictate where I can live?"

"Do you think it's only Tyler?" Ammi says. "There are hundreds like him, thousands who don't want immigrants, refugees,

Muslims, any of us coming into this country. Even the federal government is trying their best to make it harder for us."

"You'll be fighting for the rest of your life, beta," Abbu says. "And it will still not change the hearts and minds of people like that."

Even though, on a basic level, I completely understand that my parents will always want to protect me, I'm angry that they want me to give up. But maybe I'm also angry because, on a deeper level, I know what they're saying is true. Even if I somehow manage to stop two people, hundreds, maybe thousands, more will take their place. I see it every day, at school and online. The hatred is palpable, and people are no longer shy or reluctant to express their true feelings. Racists are becoming more emboldened every day, and it's not just in Corpus Christi; it's happening all over the country. But still, I'm determined to stay strong.

"Look, beta, we can't force you to stay in Pakistan with us," Abbu says. "And it's not that we don't admire your ambition and drive. But you have to understand that as parents it's extremely difficult to watch your child suffer or be in danger."

"But if you are determined to come back here, then we'll support you," Ammi says. "We'll always support you, no matter what." She takes me in her arms and hugs me tightly. I can feel her worry and fear, but also the incredible amount of love she has for me. The thought of living half a world away from them makes me tear up again, and then we're both crying.

"Tum ma beti ki achchi jori banti hai," Abbu says with an indulgent smile. "Let me get something to mop up the floor."

217

CHAPTER FORTY-FIVE

Chloe has invited me to her house to meet her parents over brunch. I can't tell which one of us is more nervous. I wipe my sweaty hands on my jeans before ringing her doorbell. I changed my outfit multiple times before deciding on dark jeans and a cream-colored blouse with little flowers embroidered into the collar and cuffs. If it wasn't for the jeans, I'd feel like I was dressed for an interview. I braided my curly hair, leaving just a few tendrils to frame my face, and added some small gold hoops to complete the outfit.

The door opens, and Chloe's standing there with a stupid grin on her face.

"I'm sorry, but we're not hiring right now," she says.

"Shut up, I didn't know what else to wear."

A woman wearing a floral-print dress appears beside Chloe and smiles.

"You must be Zara," she says. "Please come in."

Her dark hair is threaded with gray and her eyes crinkle in the corners just like Chloe's. It's like I'm looking at an older version of Chloe.

"It's very nice to meet you, Mrs. Murphy," I say. "Thank you for inviting me."

"Oh, it's our pleasure," she says. "And you can call me Patricia."

I smile politely, but I'm not at all comfortable calling a grown woman, my mother's age, by her first name. I was taught to call all adults either aunty or uncle. All desi people I know do that. I call my non-desi friends' parents either Mr. or Mrs. *Something*, but I never use their first names.

But I don't want to cause any awkwardness with Chloe's parents, so even if her mom wants me to call her Nefertiti, I will.

We go into the living room, and her father is there reading his paper. He looks up when we walk in and comes to stand next to his wife.

"I'm Joshua," he says, "and you must be Zara."

We exchange pleasantries, and soon we're all sitting around the dining table, where a variety of dishes have been neatly arranged. There's frittata and eggs Benedict and hash browns and fruit. My stomach groans loud enough to betray my hunger.

The food is delicious, and Chloe's parents seem like really nice people. Except I know how they really feel about Chloe and me. The conversation is extremely benign, and it's strange that we're all pretending to ignore the massive rainbow elephant in the room. The whole thing makes me realize that some people would rather live in a state of denial than accept the fact that their children are who they are.

"So what are your plans after high school?" Chloe's father asks.

I put my coffee cup down slowly.

"Well, I had planned to apply to a few schools out east, but it looks like I might have to reconsider my options."

"Oh?" Chloe's mom is holding her cup in midair, her pinkie finger pointed at a perfect forty-five-degree angle. Do people really do that?

"There have been some issues with our green card application," I say. "So things are a little up in the air right now."

"I see," Joshua says. "That's unfortunate."

As Chloe's parents sit silently and marinate in their white privilege, I wish desperately for this awkwardness to end.

Thankfully, Chloe suggests that we take a walk around the lake behind her house, and I quickly agree.

"So, that was nice," I say once we've crossed the street and walked into the park area.

"If by *nice* you mean *freaking weird*, then yes, I agree," Chloe says.

"It wasn't that bad," I say. "They were very nice."

"That's sweet of you to say. But just before you got here, they were telling me they don't understand how your parents are okay with you being bisexual."

"Why, because we're Muslim?"

She nods. "I'm sorry, I shouldn't even be telling you this."

"No, it's fine," I say. "It's not your fault your parents think like that."

"It just makes me so mad. They're such hypocrites."

"At least they're making an effort. And things have been getting better with the counseling and everything, haven't they?"

"I guess," she says with a sigh. "But fundamentally they'll never change, I know that."

"Do you really think so?"

"All signs point to YES. I'm just glad I'll be going away to college next year so I don't have to deal with the awkwardness anymore."

"Well, you'll still visit though, won't you?" I say.

"I guess, but I can only imagine how uncomfortable family holidays will be for me."

• • •

Nick comes over after dinner, and we take Zorro for a walk.

"So, are you really going to leave?" he says after we've walked in silence for a bit.

"Doesn't look like I have much of a choice," I say.

I stop to pick up a small stone and hurl it out in front of me. It sails over the water before falling in, and I watch as the ripples slowly move out.

He raises his arm, and I step under it to rest my head on his chest. I'm going to miss him so much it hurts to even think about it.

"I mean . . . we *could* get married."

I pull back and look up at him, fully expecting to see a grin on his face. But he looks dead serious.

"Ha-ha, very funny, Nick," I say, shaking my head at him.

"I'm not joking," he says. "If we got married, you would get your green card and you wouldn't be forced to leave the country."

"We're *seventeen*, Nick."

"In Texas, we can legally get married as long as we have parental consent. *Annnnd* you know your parents love me." He grins, and I don't know what to do with him.

"Nick, you're sweet. Hilarious but sweet."

"Look, I know it won't be the real thing. Obviously, you're dating Chloe. And you know how I feel about Priya. But she thinks this is a great idea."

I stare at him. "You actually told Priya? Are you stupid?"

"I think what you're *trying* to say is that I'm a genius. It's the

221

perfect solution. You'd get to stay, *and* Priya is in on the whole thing."

"You'd really do that for me?" I turn to look him in the eyes.

"You're my best friend, Zara," he says softly. "I'd do anything for you."

I lean in and kiss him on the cheek.

"I know," I say, hooking my arm in his. "But I still think you're an idiot."

CHAPTER FORTY-SIX

It's November, and I'm scrambling to keep up with schoolwork and college applications as winter break looms ever closer.

I've decided to apply to universities both here in the states and in Pakistan. If I get a scholarship offer, along with a spot here, then I can change my visa status and remain in the US as a student. But that's not for sure, so I've also sent off applications to a couple of universities in Karachi that have an international relations program.

I feel more at peace, now that I have a plan of action. But every little thing I do has a sense of finality to it, as if it's the last time I'll ever get to do it. Time spent with Chloe has become a precious commodity, and we both know it even though we try not to talk about it.

Leaving Zorro behind with Nick is going to be the hardest thing of all, and I know his family will take good care of him, but now, every time he jumps into my arms, my heart breaks a little more. I'm going to miss being woken up every morning by him jumping onto my bed and nudging me with his cold, wet nose until I get up and play with him.

The Monday before Thanksgiving, I walk into the living room and see Abbu and Ammi standing up close to the TV, eyes glued to the screen. Senator Delgado is being interviewed by a reporter about a potential bomb threat targeting her offices in San Antonio. No one has been arrested in association with the planned attack yet, but an anonymous online anti-immigrant group did claim responsibility before posting its manifesto all over social media.

It only takes a few seconds to find on my phone since it's already trending. This is their direct response to the speech Senator Delgado gave at the rally a few weeks ago, and they mention me and my family by name, along with dozens of other activists and Dreamers who helped organize the event. I can't even imagine the devastation such an attack would have caused.

I hear a noise outside and go to the window. I push the curtains aside slightly and gasp.

"What is it, Zara?" Ammi says.

"Reporters." I do a quick count. "At least a dozen of them. And vans too."

"They must be here because of the attack," Abbu says.

"What should we do?" I ask.

"Call that Ms. Anderson," Ammi says. "Maybe she can help."

I call but it goes straight to voice mail. She's probably swamped dealing with their own chaos. Next I try Shireen Khala, who answers right away and promises to come over immediately.

"How did you get here without the reporters seeing you?" I ask as soon as she's knocking on the back door.

"I parked a block away and walked through your neighbor's backyard."

"Shireen, can you do something about all this?" Ammi says.

She's not taking this well, nervously pacing up and down the living room floor.

"Let me go out and talk to them. I'll tell them you have no comment."

She steps outside and is immediately swarmed by reporters, who stick their microphones and cell phones in her face. I watch discreetly through the window, and I'm in awe of how calm and composed she is as she tells them that she's our lawyer and that we have no comment at the moment and to please respect our privacy.

Unfortunately, this does not make them leave. In fact, it looks like they're now planning to camp out in our front yard.

Shireen Khala comes back inside just as the phone rings. It's Ms. Anderson.

"Zara, I'm sorry I missed your call. I assume you've seen the news?"

"I have. Is everyone there okay?"

"Yes, but it's a zoo here right now. Senator Delgado wanted me to bring you all here, just to be safe. We're sending a car for you."

"Okay, but what should we do about all the reporters in front of our house?"

"Don't say anything until you've spoken to Senator Delgado," Ms. Anderson says urgently.

"Our lawyer already told them we have no comment."

"Okay, good. Please bring her along if possible."

"Of course, and please ask the driver to come to our neighbor's house. I'll text you the address right now."

As soon as I hang up, I send her directions and tell Ammi and Abbu to pack an overnight bag each. Then I call Nick while I pack my own stuff. He'll see the reporters any minute now and worry.

"Nick, can you take Zorro? Senator Delgado is sending a car for us and wants us to stay somewhere safe."

"Oh my God, are you guys okay?" he says.

"Yes, we're fine, but I need you to come to the back door and grab Zorro."

He's here in minutes and gives us all big hugs.

"My parents said to call them if you need anything at all. They'll keep an eye out here and let you know if the reporters leave," he says before slipping out the back with Zorro and a few of his favorite toys.

The car service arrives soon after, and all of us pile in. The driver takes us to a very nice hotel in San Antonio where Senator Delgado and Ms. Anderson are waiting for us. They usher us through the lobby to our suite and ask us to meet them in one of the conference rooms downstairs after we've freshened up.

When we go back down, they're waiting for us with refreshments.

"I'm so sorry you're in this situation," she says once we're sitting down. "I feel responsible for drawing attention to you. How can I help?"

"You already helped us by expediting our green card process, Senator Delgado," Ammi says. "We're very grateful that you're helping our daughter."

"Hopefully those reporters will get tired of waiting and leave soon," Abbu says.

"I'm just glad that no one got hurt," I say. "I read the manifesto online. I can't believe some of the things that were on it. Have they caught the people responsible yet?"

"They're working on it," Senator Delgado says. "So hopefully it shouldn't be long now."

"What about all the other people that were named? Are they all safe?"

"Yes, we've arranged safe accommodation for all of them and their families until the perpetrators have been apprehended."

"It's very kind of you to do this," Ammi says. "I have to ask you, Senator Delgado, how do you deal with so much pushback and still continue with all of your work?"

"Well, Mrs. Hossain, it's precisely because of the pushback that I must keep going," Senator Delgado replies. "That's why I'm so impressed with your daughter. She refuses to stop fighting, and that's what we need from our young people."

We go back up to our rooms, and I check in with Nick to see how Zorro's doing.

"She told Ammi that she's impressed with me because I won't stop fighting," I tell him.

"How much did you have to pay her to say that?" he quips.

"Shut up, Nick," I say. "You're just jealous because someone thinks I'm cool for a change."

"All those reporters probably think you're cool too," he says. "I don't think they're leaving anytime soon."

"Ugh, that's great. Just what I need, when I have so many tests this week."

"I talked to your teachers this morning, and they said your safety comes first. You can always take the tests next week."

"Thanks, Nick. I should go check on my parents now. Thanks for watching Zorro."

"Call me if anything happens."

We hang up, and I lie down in bed and stare up at the ceiling. Ammi and Abbu are in the adjoining room, probably already asleep. I miss Zorro, the warmth of his little furry body pressed against mine. I wonder for the umpteenth time how someone can hate people so much that they would want them dead, simply because they look different. I want to get a look inside their collective head to find out what it is about people like me that triggers such intense feelings of hatred.

As it has done so many times over the last few months, my mind goes back to Tyler. I go over every single interaction with him in my mind. Was it something I said or did? Did I somehow make him feel inadequate or cheated? I've heard the comments before. About how all the immigrants were taking all the spots in colleges and universities with their superior SAT scores and AP courses and high GPAs. A girl I peer-tutored at school claimed that she didn't do well on a math test because the Asian students took all the high marks. She'd make fun of them because they studied so much and never did anything else. I remember wanting to ask her what exactly was stopping her from studying just as hard. But I already knew her answer to that.

That was the reason people like her resented us. Because we worked hard and pushed ourselves. I can't recall ever seeing Tyler actually pay attention in class. He was obsessed with football and the popularity it garnered him. So maybe that's why he hated me. Or maybe it was just that when he looked at me, he saw something he didn't like. A brown face with a Muslim name.

I have spent so much time and energy going over this in my head lately, but I remember: The problem doesn't lie with me. He's the one with the problem, the one who doesn't want to coexist with people who aren't exactly like him.

I think about Tyler's father. The lengths to which people like him will go to hurt others has convinced me that there *is* something inherently evil at play. How do I deal with someone who's convinced that his right to exist in this world trumps mine?

CHAPTER FORTY-SEVEN

We stay in the hotel for the next couple of days. Nick says the number of reporters outside our house has dwindled, but a couple are still there. I'm getting worried about all the schoolwork I'm missing, but on the plus side, I've been able to shadow Senator Delgado all day, watching her as she works to push her immigration reforms through. It's a real-life lesson in politics and social justice, more valuable than anything I'd be learning at school.

On the third morning, Nick calls to say that the reporters have all left. They've pestered all our neighbors with no success, and seeing no signs of our return, they've moved on to the next story.

As we're getting ready to head back to Corpus, Senator Delgado asks us to stay for lunch.

"I may have some good news for you," she says over salad and grilled salmon. "I may have a way for Zara to stay. But I didn't want to say anything until it was all approved, in case it fell through."

My face lights up, and I almost jump up to hug her. But I manage to restrain myself.

"Dr. Hossain, I have a proposition for you," she says. "If you are interested, I'd like to bring you on as my campaign's private physician. We'll be hitting the road for the midterms very soon, and I would be honored to have a health professional with your level of experience on hand for the team. Fully sponsored, of course."

We stare at her in stunned silence.

"Well, don't all of you speak at once," she says with a smile.

"May we have some time to think about it?" Abbu finally manages to say.

"Of course, please take some time to talk it over," she says, bustling out of the room when one of her assistants knocks on the door.

We don't say much during the car ride home, not wanting to talk about this in front of the driver. But as soon as we enter our house, I can't hold it in any longer.

"So?" I ask with the biggest smile on my face. "Isn't this perfect?"

Ammi smiles and gives me a big hug. "It is very good news, beta. But—"

"But nothing, Ammi. Please, this would solve all our problems."

"Does it really, Zara? Think about what you're saying."

"Actually, beta," Abbu says quietly, "nothing has changed. A short time ago, I was shot. And now we've been chased out of our own home by reporters because of a bomb threat that some lunatic planned with our family in mind. My family. Do you get that, Zara?" His voice has risen until he's nearly shouting the last part, and I cringe. Abbu has rarely ever raised his voice at me or Ammi.

"Please, Zara," Ammi says. "Your father has been through

enough. We've all been through enough, and I don't know how much more I can take."

In that moment, I realize just how selfish I've been lately, and I'm instantly overcome with guilt.

"I'm sorry, Abbu," I say, putting my arms around his middle. "I've just been so caught up in my own stuff."

"I understand, beta," Abbu says, stroking my hair, all signs of anger gone. "I know it'll be a big sacrifice for you if you come back with us."

"But we simply cannot stand to be here any longer," Ammi says.

I know there's nothing I can say to convince them otherwise, so I don't say anything. Ammi resumes her packing and Abbu goes to take a nap, so I decide to go over to Nick's to pick up Zorro.

"What's wrong?" Nick says as soon as he opens the door.

"Senator Delgado offered Abbu a job so that we could all stay, but my parents still want to leave," I say.

"Are you serious?" He hands me Zorro's leash as we start walking toward Cole Park.

"I wish I wasn't," I say. "They're just so adamant about leaving, they won't even listen to me."

"But this would literally solve all your problems, right?"

"Exactly. And I know it's been so hard and terrifying, what happened, but still. I wish they'd see my side of things."

"So, what are you going to do?" Nick says.

"I have no idea," I say with a big sigh. "If Abbu's visa doesn't get extended, then there's no way I can stay."

"There has to be some way to convince your parents," he says. "I'll get mine to talk to them."

"I'm willing to try anything at this point."

• • •

Back at home, we have company. It's Shireen Khala, and I've never been happier to see anyone in my life.

When I walk in, she's chatting with Ammi and Abbu over tea and dessert.

"Iqbal Bhai, if the senator is giving you this opportunity, then you have to take it," she says. I could kiss her. "Why are you even thinking about it?"

"It's not that simple, Shireen," Abbu says. "After everything that's happened, I don't know how we'd ever feel safe here again."

"These days nowhere is really safe," she says. "Do you think you won't be in any danger in Pakistan? There is so much political instability there—how can you be sure it's any better?"

"At least we'll be among our friends and family," Ammi says.

"You have family here, Nilufer Baji," Shireen Khala says gently. "I am your family. Isabella and John are your family."

"Yes, of course," Abbu says. "But we shouldn't have to feel like we constantly have a target on our backs."

"But what about Zara? Do you think she'll be safe over there? If anyone finds out she's queer, she could be in grave danger. You know this."

"She doesn't have to tell anyone over there," Ammi says. "Shireen, this is a personal matter."

"Do you honestly think it won't come out eventually? What if she meets someone and wants to get married? Then what?"

Ammi and Abbu are both silent. They have no good answer to this question. It's one I haven't been able to ask them, because much as I'm desperate to stay, I don't want to force them to if they're going to be unhappy.

Shireen Khala turns to Abbu. "Iqbal Bhai, you only have to

do this until you all get your green cards. After that, if you and Baji still want, you can go back. But at least Zara will be off at some Ivy League university by then. If you leave now, you're risking her future."

Abbu looks at me, his eyes welling up. "I don't want to do anything that will hurt her future, Shireen. She's my only child, and I would do anything for her. But I'm afraid these people will come after us again. And what if she was the one who got shot? What if she's at home next time they come to our house? How am I supposed to keep her safe?" He breaks down in sobs, and I can't bear it. I run to him and cradle him in my arms like a child. Ammi is right next to me crying too.

"Abbu, it's okay," I say to him softly, wiping his tears. "You don't have to stay here for me. I'll come with you, and I'll get into a good college in Karachi. Everything will be fine. I promise."

He's shaking his head. "Nahin, beta, I can't let you do that."

"It's okay, Abbu. It's not worth losing our peace of mind over."

"What kind of father lets his own child sacrifice her future for her parents?" He looks at me, and there is so much pain in his eyes that I would do anything to make it go away. Having to go to a school in a different country is nothing compared to seeing my parents suffer like this. I won't be the reason my parents can't sleep at night.

"Nahin, Zara," Ammi says. "Abbu is right. We can take measures to stay safe. We can put in a security system and whatever else we have to do to feel safe. And Shireen is right. After we get our green cards and you've gone away to college, we can go back if we still want."

"But, Ammi, what about—"

233

"Nothing, beta." Ammi is adamant now. "I became so consumed with my own fears that I forgot what is most important to us."

"After all, we came to this country to give you a better future," Abbu says. "So how can we leave now, when it's so close? You've worked so hard all your life, Zara. We couldn't ask for a more perfect daughter, so we'll do whatever it takes to make sure you accomplish everything you want."

Now I'm the one who's sobbing uncontrollably. As always, my parents will do anything for my happiness, and I can never repay them. All I can do is make them as proud as I can and make sure I don't squander the opportunities they've given me.

Even Shireen Khala has tears running down her cheeks, although she's smiling.

"I just came here for some chai and your delicious cookies, Nilufer Baji. Now I feel like I'm in the middle of a Bollywood movie."

Abbu walks over to her and bends to kiss her forehead.

"Shireen, I have to hand it to you," he says with a broad smile. "You're a really great lawyer, haan. You even convinced your stubborn older brother to see reason."

"Iqbal Bhai, you're embarrassing me," Shireen Khala says. "In this country, _you_ all are my family. I only want the best for you."

I step forward and give her a tight hug.

"Thank you," I whisper in her ear.

"You know I always have your back, Zara," she whispers in reply.

"Okay, so it's decided," Abbu says. "Tomorrow morning, I'll call Senator Delgado to accept her offer, and Zara can help us unpack all these boxes." He smiles at me, and it's as if a huge weight has been lifted off me.

I can't wait to tell Nick and Chloe, but I'm suddenly exhausted, the stress of the last few days finally sinking in. And the more I think about it, the more it doesn't feel right. My parents are doing this for me; they're going against their own best interest. And that is something I'm not sure I can live with. I rack my brain for a solution that will work for us all, but deep in the pit of my stomach, I worry there's really no such possibility.

CHAPTER FORTY-EIGHT

The next few days pass in sort of a haze as I vacillate between being relieved there is light at the end of the tunnel and feeling guilty because that light will bring my parents pain and discomfort. I know Abbu only agreed to accept the offer for my sake, and I cannot watch my father swallow his pride and work for the senator, knowing that all the hard work and dedication he put into his practice of the last fourteen years of his life meant nothing. I cannot bear for him to look at himself in the mirror and feel anything other than pride in what he's doing. And I cannot live with myself, knowing that just for me my mother chose to stay in a country where she'll be afraid every time her husband steps out the door. Where someone could be waiting in the shadows, ready to tear it all down again.

Sure, I'd get to be around my friends for the rest of senior year and live the life I want, but at what cost?

I find myself lying to everyone about how I'm feeling. My parents assume that I'm ecstatic, as do my friends. But honestly, I'm torn apart and I can't see a way out.

It's been days since I've been able to sleep properly, and the stress is starting to show. I'm irritable and snapping at everyone. Then, early one morning, as I'm retrieving Zorro's ball from underneath the recliner, I find something glittery hiding there as well.

It's my cousin's wedding invitation. I see it, and something clicks in my mind.

The answer is right in front of me, and it's perfect.

How did I not think about this before?

I rush to my parents' bedroom. They're still asleep, but I've decided that it's time for them to wake up.

I shake Ammi gently, but she's so nervous these days that she screams and almost gives Abbu a heart attack. They both sit up and give me dirty looks.

"What is it, Zara?" Ammi asks. "Are you all right?"

"Yes. I've had a brilliant idea," I say triumphantly.

"And this brilliant idea couldn't wait until, say, breakfast?" Abbu asks, rubbing his eyes.

"You don't understand," I say impatiently. "It's the perfect solution."

"Okay, so let's hear it," Ammi says.

"Canada," I say, standing tall and proud.

"Okay?" Abbu says. They both look at me blankly.

"We can go to Canada. And stay with Murshed Uncle."

I can tell by the looks on their faces that it's starting to dawn on them that their daughter is a bona fide genius.

"Isn't it brilliant?" I ask.

"Did you get any sleep at all?" Ammi asks.

"Who cares about sleep, Ammi? Didn't you hear what I said?"

"But I thought we agreed that I would work for the senator," Abbu said. "Why did you change your mind again?"

"Abbu, I know you're only doing it for me," I said. "And I just can't let you two do that."

"But what about your friends?" Ammi says. "And your life over here?"

"Canada isn't that far. And my friends and my life here are important, yes. But not more than you."

"You know, Murshed has been asking me for years to move over there, closer to him and his family," Abbu says.

"He said it's a lot better there," Ammi says. "Especially compared to the way things are here these days."

"So, you think you'll do it?" I'm practically buzzing with excitement.

Ammi and Abbu look at each other.

"I think we should definitely look into it," Abbu says.

I hug them both and run back to my room to start some online research.

When it's a reasonable waking hour, I call Shireen Khala, and she's surprised to hear what I have to say.

"I didn't know you were still thinking about all of this," she says. "I thought it was a done deal with the senator."

"It wasn't sitting right with me," I tell her. "You've seen how stressed Ammi has been these last couple of months. I don't want her to feel unsafe all the time and worry about our safety."

"Well, it sounds like a pretty good idea," Shireen Khala says. "I'll look into it too, in case you need some help with the paperwork."

It feels right. A place where they have what they want—family and safety—and I can have what I want—freedom, equality . . . and family.

Now I just have to share the news with Chloe, Nick, and Priya and hope they'll understand.

CHAPTER FORTY-NINE

I'm sitting across from Nick and Priya at Scoopz. Now that I know about them being a couple, they're nauseatingly cute with each other, sharing a bowl of frozen yogurt. I guess I get to eat all my sour gummies alone from now on. I've just told them about the change of plans, and they're a little stunned.

"We've never even talked about Canada," Nick says. "How did you even come up with that plan?"

"Do you remember my cousin Ayesha? From Vancouver?"

"Yes," Nick says. "She was really pretty."

Priya snatches the spoon from him, and I grin at them.

"Anyway . . . I found this wedding invitation they sent us a while back, and that must have triggered something in my genius brain."

Nick mumbles into his frozen yogurt.

"But *why* did you change your mind?" Priya asks.

I tell her what my parents had said right before Shireen Khala guilted them into agreeing to stay.

"Yeah, I get that," Priya says. "I wouldn't want them doing that for me either. It's too much."

"I'm going to miss you," Nick says. "Canada's so far."

"I'll buy you a map," I say.

"Now we'll have an excuse to visit," Priya says.

I'm glad they're taking the news so well because I'm not looking forward to telling Chloe.

● ● ●

"What? I thought you'd decided that you could stay here," she says. "Didn't the senator offer your father a job?"

So I go through the whole spiel again.

"I know it's going to be difficult, but it's not that far," I say. "It's like a five-hour plane ride from Houston."

"I get it," she says, but she sounds so sad that I can't bear it.

"You know, you could apply to some universities in Vancouver as well," I say. "Then we could still be together."

"I *am* dying to get out of here," she says. "I mean, things with my parents still aren't great, so it might be better to get away somewhere else for a while."

This is going so much better than I'd anticipated, and that only convinces me that this is the right thing to do.

● ● ●

The next few weeks fly by as we apply for permanent residency in Canada. It's still a lengthy process, but because my father is a physician, we anticipate that it won't take too long. In the meantime, he has agreed to work for Senator Delgado until we get our Canadian papers.

As the end of the year approaches, my friends and I can't help but stress about our college applications. I've researched a handful of universities in Canada, and I'm excited to apply. But I have to wait until I get my Canadian permanent resident status before I can submit any applications, so I plan to volunteer with Senator Delgado until then. And Chloe is applying to a few of the same Canadian universities as me.

Nick and Priya plan to stay near Corpus Christi, so it's a relief to know that we'll each only be a plane ride away. We're already planning trips to meet up, and things feel good again.

• • •

Ammi and Abbu have decided that a huge going-away party is a great way to start our new adventure. Abbu is running some last-minute errands while Ammi and I put the finishing touches on the kheer and sevaiyyan. I'm wearing a new churidar set that I've been saving for a special occasion. It's a beautiful lilac georgette with tiny pearls embroidered into the flowers at the neckline and the sleeves. I love how the kameez flows around my ankles, and I'm admiring my silver anklets and matching toe rings, when the doorbell rings. It's Chloe. She's wearing a pretty purple lace blouse and black high-waisted jeans. Her normally straight hair is carefully curled, and when I hug her, I'm enveloped by the scent of lavender and honey. The mehndi I applied to her hands last night has come out really well. It's a dark brown against her fair skin and I'm really proud of the paisley pattern I did on her.

"Did you dab it with lemon water?" I ask.

"Yes, whenever it started to dry out, just like you said," she replies. "Isn't it so pretty?" She holds out her palms for me to admire. "I love what you're wearing, by the way." She steps back to get a better look. "I love this color on you."

Ammi walks in just then.

"Hello, Chloe," Ammi says, giving her a kiss on the cheek. "Your mehndi looks gorgeous."

"Thank you," Chloe says. "And my parents send their regards. They're sorry they couldn't make it."

"I'm sorry they couldn't join us. Okay, now come with me," she says. "You have to taste all the food." She goes off into the kitchen, and we follow her. "So, what would you like to try first, Chloe?"

"It all looks so good I don't even know where to begin." Chloe looks at me for help.

"Try the zarda first," I say. "Ammi just finished making it, so it's nice and hot." I pick up a bowl from the pretty floral set that Ammi brought with her from Pakistan and only uses on special occasions. I put a few spoonfuls of the sweet, cardamom-infused yellow rice in it and hand it to Chloe.

"Oh my God, it's delicious," she says after a taste.

"Okay, so now try it with this cold kheer." I put a few spoons of the rice pudding on top of the zarda and watch her closely.

"Mmm, it's so good."

"Isn't it the best?" I grab a bowl for myself, and for the next few minutes, we relish the sweetness together.

"I made shaami kabab and paranthay for lunch," Ammi says. "I made a few special ones for Chloe," she adds.

"She means they're not spicy," I whisper to Chloe with a wink.

"Ah, yes, always worried about the white girl," Chloe says with a grin.

"Well, you can try the spicy ones, but don't come crying to me when your mouth is on fire," I say.

"Maybe I can try a bite of yours and if I don't combust then I can have some more," she says.

"And there's always raita to cool it off."

"Is that the yogurt salad I had that one time?"

"Yes, it helps to quench the fire."

We help Ammi set out all the food and dishes in anticipation of the visitors, who should start arriving soon.

Shireen Khala is the first, followed soon by a few other

Pakistani families that we know from the mosque and cultural center.

When my parents first moved here, they made sure to socialize as much as possible with the local Pakistani community, especially when Abbu worked long hours at the hospital as a new resident. I remember many weekends when Ammi and I would go to some aunty's house or another on weekends and spend the day. I'd play with the other kids, and the grown-ups would chat and watch old Bollywood movies together. There was always good food and lots of fun and games.

But things began to change as the other kids my age and I got older. Some families were more conservative and orthodox while others, like mine, were a bit more liberal when it came to parenting. So, while some of us got to do sleepovers and go to parties, others weren't allowed to do any of that. Resentments grew and things were said, which led to missed invitations to gatherings, and by the time I was around fifteen, my parents' social circle had grown a lot smaller. But they liked it that way because they preferred the company of like-minded individuals who were part of their friends' group. I too was relieved not to face the awkwardness of having to explain why I didn't fast during Ramadan and why I didn't pray five times a day. My parents taught me to question everything I learned about religion and to explore my relationship with God as I got older, so I developed a healthy curiosity about all organized religion. But sometimes I wondered if my parents didn't secretly miss having more social interaction with people who shared similar upbringing and roots. Especially now that I know they would both rather move back to Pakistan than fight to remain here, I have to question a lot of the assumptions I've made over the years about their lives.

By the time Abbu is back, most of our guests are here. I'm

super excited because Ammi's made haleem after a long time. It's a spicy stew made with wheat, barley, and other grains, and it's one of my favorite foods. That and dahi vada, which is chilling in the fridge. People are still coming in, and I introduce Chloe to a couple of my desi childhood friends. There's Abbas and Zakia, twins whom I first met during Friday-afternoon Arabic lessons at the mosque. They're our age, and soon we're chatting about upcoming college admission woes.

Nick and his parents come a little later, and so do Priya and her parents.

Once most of the other guests have left, Abbu breaks out the karaoke machine.

As I watch my friends and family singing and laughing together, I feel a pang of regret, because I know that all of this will change soon. But if the events of the last couple of months have shown me anything, it's that I can withstand a lot, as long as the people I love are by my side. And as I look toward my future, it looks bright and promising once again, filled with all their love and support. I know I will need it as I fight for change. And I know I will never stop fighting.

AUTHOR'S NOTE

First of all, thank you for reading Zara's story. Like the Hossains, my family spent years waiting for our green cards. But then someone else's clerical error derailed the entire process and we were asked to go back home. That was when we realized that the United States—the place where my husband and I had started our married lives, where our children were born and had taken their first steps, and where we had dreamed about our future—had never really been our home. With broken hearts, we packed up our lives and moved to Canada to start over.

The precariousness of the Hossain family's immigration status is a permanent fixture in the everyday lives of many immigrants in the US today, and Zara struggles to feel what so many others seem to take for granted: a sense of belonging.

When I sat down to write this book, I knew I wanted it to be about those of us who had the courage to leave behind everything we knew and start new lives in foreign countries. About those of us who keep fighting to make space for ourselves in a country where some will always see us as the "other," where our hard work and contributions may never be acknowledged, but where, nonetheless, we have managed to carve out lives worthy of respect and pride.

In today's political climate, it is crucial that we all come together as allies to stand up against racism and fight injustice when we see it. I hope that Zara's indomitable spirit and her refusal to give up have inspired you to resist and push back against the intolerance and prejudice that continue to threaten immigrant families and destroy lives.

ACKNOWLEDGMENTS

Though this past year has been quite challenging, I chose to focus on remembering the many wonderful individuals I met, both virtually and in person, during my debut year and how their kindness and generosity filled me with positivity and confidence as I worked on this book. There are so many people who I'm thankful for.

First and foremost, my agent, Hillary Jacobson, who tirelessly champions all my work and helps me through the tough times. I am so thankful to have you in my corner. My amazing editor, Jeffrey West, who sees right into the heart of my stories, thank you for your insight and for helping me shape my writing into something I can be very proud of. David Levithan, I'm deeply grateful for your support of my work and for notes and comments that always make me smile.

My entire Scholastic family: Maeve Norton and Elizabeth Parisi, who create the most beautiful covers for my books; Elisabeth Ferrari, publicist extraordinaire; Josh Berlowitz and Melissa Schirmer, who helped keep this book on schedule; Elizabeth Whiting, Savannah D'Amico, and the rest of the Sales team; Lizette Serrano, Rachel Feld, Emily Heddleson, Danielle Yadao, Shannon Pender, Lauren Donovan, Shelly Romero, and Nikki Mutch, it was an absolute delight to spend time with you all last year. Thank you for making each event so memorable for me.

My Scholastic Canada family: Nikole Kritikos, Allie Chenoweth, Erin Haggett, Maral Maclagan, and Susan Travis, thank you for all the support and for just being the loveliest people. I can't wait for karaoke night!

The sweetest, most talented, and all-around best people, my fellow Scholastic authors who made my debut year so joyful and fun: Bill Konigsberg, Lamar Giles, Jennifer Donnelly, Aida Salazar, and Sayantani DasGupta. Here's to many more events together.

Sandhya Menon, Tanaz Bhatena, Robin Stevenson, Mason Deaver, and Julian Winters—thank you for being there through all this. Your friendship means so much!

I could not have gone through this journey without Adalyn Grace, Astrid Scholte, and Mel Howard. You know what you mean to me.

My partner in crime, Nafiza Azad, what an amazing journey we're on. I'm so thankful that I get to share it with you. Thank you for being my confidante and real-life author friend.

Rob Bittner, what can I say? I cherish our friendship and our coffee dates. So much.

My heartfelt gratitude to all the teachers and librarians who support our stories and get them into the hands of readers. To all the bloggers and reviewers, thank you for everything you do. And the biggest thanks to all the readers whose support fuels us to write more stories.

I wouldn't be living this dream if it weren't for my husband and my two daughters, whose unwavering love and support makes all this possible.

And last but certainly not least, eternal gratitude to my mother, who sat patiently by when I was first learning English and fostered my love for reading and writing in the process.

ABOUT THE AUTHOR

Sabina Khan writes about Muslim teens who straddle cultures. Her debut novel, *The Love and Lies of Rukhsana Ali,* was an Amazon Best Book of the Month and received a starred review from *School Library Journal.* Sabina was born in Germany, spent her teens in Bangladesh, and lived in Macao, Illinois, and Texas before settling down in British Columbia with her husband, two daughters, and the best puppy in the world. Visit her online at sabina-khan.com and on Twitter at @Sabina_Writer.

Don't miss Sabina Khan's latest novel!

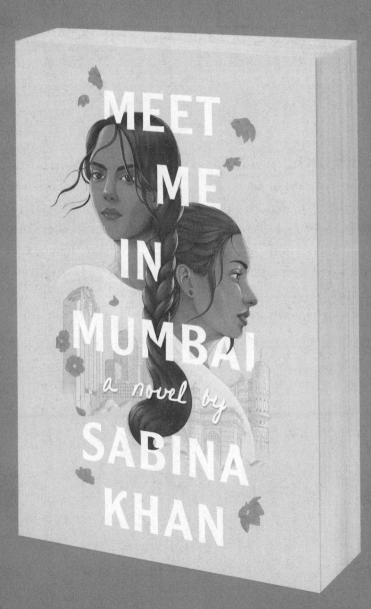

MEET ME IN MUMBAI

a novel by

SABINA KHAN

IreadYA.com